HAZEL HOLT

MRS. MALORY
DETECTIVE IN RESIDENCE

A SIGNET BOOK

SIGNET
Published by the Penguin Group
Penguin Books USA Inc., 375 Hudson Street,
New York, New York 10014, U.S.A.
Penguin Books Ltd, 27 Wrights Lane,
London W8 5TZ, England
Penguin Books Australia Ltd, Ringwood,
Victoria, Australia
Penguin Books Canada Ltd, 10 Alcorn Avenue,
Toronto, Ontario, Canada M4V 3B2
Penguin Books (N.Z.) Ltd, 182–190 Wairau Road,
Auckland 10, New Zealand

Penguin Books Ltd, Registered Offices:
Harmondsworth, Middlesex, England

Published by Signet, an imprint of Dutton Signet,
a division of Penguin Books USA Inc.
Previously published in a Dutton edition.

First Signet Printing, December, 1995
10 9 8 7 6 5 4 3 2 1

 REGISTERED TRADEMARK—MARCA REGISTRADA

Printed in the United States of America

PUBLISHER'S NOTE
This is a work of fiction. Names, characters, places, and incidents either
are the product of the author's imagination or are used fictitiously,
and any resemblance to actual persons, living or dead, events, or locales
is entirely coincidental.

For Natalie

Death is a word not to be declined in any case.

1

"Are you sure you'll be all right?" I asked.

"Yes, Ma," Michael replied in the patient tone of one who has already answered this particular question several times before.

"There's enough stuff in the freezer for you and the animals for a month; after that they'll have to have tins. And Rosemary said she's always happy to give you a meal; just phone and say when."

"Yes, Ma."

"Oh, and the phone bill's due sometime this month. Can you pay it?"

"*Yes*, Ma."

"Now are you sure I've left you enough money to see you through until I get back?"

"I'm sure you have."

I caught Michael's eye, and we both laughed.

"Yes, I know," I said. "Don't fuss."

"I didn't say a word."

We were sitting in some discomfort at a very small table cluttered with used coffee cups at

Heathrow. All around us loudspeakers were disseminating what was doubtless vital information about flight times in muffled and unintelligible tones to the crowds of would-be travelers, crouched protectively over their luggage. There had recently been another bomb scare, and here and there, among all the people milling about, I saw, with a sense of shock, soldiers with rifles and sniffer dogs.

"Goodness," I said, "look at that sweet dog! I wonder how they train them?"

Michael very rightly ignored this question and said, "Do you want another cup of coffee?"

"No, thanks, I'm nervous enough already without any more stimulants! How about you? Can you manage another Danish pastry?"

"No, I'm fine," he replied.

"Are you sure?" I persisted. "It's a long drive back; you'll be hungry."

"If I'm hungry, I'll stop and get something on the way."

"Yes, of course—sorry, love."

"Carry on." Michael grinned. "You've got to use up all the fussing and fretting you would have spread over four whole months."

"Oh, dear," I said, "it does sound an awfully long time. I wish I weren't going."

"Nonsense," Michael said bracingly, "you'll love it when you get there. The time'll fairly *whiz* by and you won't want to come back."

"Oh, yes, I know," I replied, "you're absolutely right. It's just the *going* that's so awful!"

I opened my handbag to check for the umpteenth time that my tickets and passport were safely there and said, "I think I'll go through now. There's no need for you to hang about, and I'd like you to get back to Taviscombe before dark."

"Are you sure?" he asked. "It seems a bit unfriendly."

"I'll have a nice read," I said. At the barrier I blinked hard to keep back the tears I knew would embarrass him.

"Have a lovely peaceful time without me," I said, "and Jack and Rosemary are there if you need anything."

"I shall probably have wild parties every night or turn the house into a gambling hell. Have a lovely time and take mega-care."

It was with some reluctance that I had left my West Country home to travel across the Atlantic, but continual nagging from my old friend Linda Kowolski had led me to accept an invitation from the chair (such an extraordinary title) of her faculty to spend a term (semester?—I hoped the language barrier wasn't going to prove insurmountable) at Wilmot, her college in Pennsylvania, teaching a course on lesser-known nineteenth-century British women writers.

"It would be part of the women's studies course," Linda had explained. "Marge Ellis, who normally teaches it, will be away on a sabbatical in the fall."

"I don't think I know anything about women's studies," I said doubtfully.

"Yes, you do," she affirmed positively. "It's what you do all the time; it's just that you've never *thought* of it that way before."

Nevertheless, as I opened my file of notes in an attempt to distract my mind from the fact that we were thirty thousand feet over the Atlantic, I wondered if the material I had prepared on Mrs. Oliphant, Mary Cholmondeley, and Charlotte M. Yonge was sufficiently feminist for the young adherents of the women's movement I would be faced with.

"And I don't really know the *jargon*," I had said helplessly. "You know how I loathe structuralism or—what's it called?—deconstructionism and all that nonsense."

"That's *fine*." Linda's voice across the Atlantic telephone was positively *vibrant* with enthusiasm. "Just what they need: a refreshing dose of proper, old-fashioned lit crit—the sort of thing *we* can't hope to get away with. We *have* to teach theory! Think of it. Only from you can those poor kids get any idea of what literature is *really* about— I mean, *enjoyment*, actually reading for pleasure. Come and amaze them!"

So here I was, nervously preparing to do just that.

I hate flying. When I think of all that *space* underneath the plane, my knees give way, and if I should inadvertently look out of the window, my stomach turns over and I get vertigo. The 747 wasn't too full, and I'd managed to get a seat on the aisle, which helped my claustrophobia but left me prey to the itinerant drinks trolleys and the constant passage of people up and down the aisles on their way to the lavatories. I congratulated myself on being well away from the nursery section, since I had seen several carry-cots coming on board and the air of the departure lounge had been rent by the wails of toddlers who had quite sensibly decided that air travel was not for them.

Carefully avoiding the (to me) terrifying instructions about what one had to do if the plane should come down into the sea (drown?), I reached for the flight magazine and tried to lose myself in the glossy advertisements.

The stewardess crashed her trolley to a halt in the aisle and put a tray ladened with goodies before me. I can't understand people who complain about airline food. I always enjoy mine, and I have a childish delight in all those fascinating hygienically wrapped-up bits and pieces, salt and pepper and mints and little cleansing pads. Lovely. I had a Campari and soda and a little bottle of wine (Californian) *and* a Drambuie afterwards (so as not to miss out on anything) so that by the time all the trays were cleared away and everyone else was watching the movie I was really quite sleepy. The blinds were drawn over the windows and my little light wasn't working properly so I couldn't read (if they can't make the reading lights work, for God's sake, what sort of state is the *engine* in?), and gradually my eyelids drooped and I was asleep.

Linda's sister, Anna, met me at Kennedy. I was to stay a few nights at her flat in Brooklyn Heights, just to have a quick look round New York. I'd been there before some years ago with my husband, Peter, and, after he died, Anna had often tried to persuade me to come over for a visit, but somehow there had never been the opportunity until now.

I looked with amazement and admiration at the way Anna was steering the car effortlessly through the terrifying traffic that swirled about us on the Van Wyck Expressway, while keeping up a constant flow of chat. How was I, how was Michael, was that cute cat still as devilish as ever, and those darling dogs? Would I like to go out for a meal this evening? There was a wonderful new Chinese place on Henry Street that I would surely love, or was I tired? What say we phone for a pizza and watch a tape? There were millions of people who wanted to see me, but only if I wanted—though it might be nice to have a party on Saturday, the liquor store on the corner of Montague Street had a special offer on organic wine—did I know about organic wine? Everyone here was very into organic wine; there's these great vineyards in the state of Washington. . . .

I sat back and let it all flow over me until we turned into Pineapple Street and drew up in front of Anna's apartment.

"My God, there's a place to *park!*" Anna cried. "Quite unheard of—it must be your benign influence!"

The doorman greeted us absently and went back to watching his television—some musical extravaganza in Spanish on the Spanish-language channel—and we squashed into the tiny lift with one of Anna's neighbors and his large and extremely friendly basset hound.

I pleaded for a quiet evening, and so we sat around eating linguine and gorgeous American ice cream and chatting.

"I'm worried about Linda," Anna said, scooping the last spoonful of Häagen-Dazs butter pecan out of the carton. "She's working too hard—in her office until two or three every morning. She looks terrible. I tell her 'If you go on like this, you'll have a breakdown,' but she doesn't listen. She always was stubborn as a mule, just like when we were kids."

"I gather that her schedule is pretty full," I said, experimentally pronouncing it the American way.

"Yes. Her chair is a nice guy but *weak,* and there are certain members of that department who are pretty good at dodging anything that looks like hard work. It's the conscientious ones like Linda, who care about their students, who get stuck with all the extra stuff."

Anna is the elder sister. There are just the two of them now; their brother, Dan, was killed in Vietnam. Their parents died when the two youngest were still at school, and Anna, just out of college, more or less brought them up. She had been married briefly, but I gathered it hadn't worked out; she and Linda didn't speak about it, and she always seems very tough and extroverted, lively, funny, and bursting with energy. But I have seen (when she thought she wasn't observed) an expression on her face of great sadness and even, occasionally, despair.

I woke up quite early the next morning and went into the little kitchenette to make some coffee. I was touched to see that Anna had laid out a packet of bacon and some eggs for an English breakfast. As I was pouring a glass of orange juice, Anna came in. She was wearing a sweat-stained tracksuit and her hair was caught back in a wide band.

"Orange juice or coffee?" I asked.

"Juice, please," she said, and sat down on a chair and to my immense surprise reached down and removed two curved metal objects from her ankles.

"Good gracious!" I exclaimed. "What on earth are they?"

"Weights." She leaned forward and pulled up her socks. "That's better; they rub like hell!"

"What is this?" I asked. "Some kind of medieval torture?"

"Sort of. No, the extra weight helps sweat off the pounds—and, brother, do I have a way to go!"

Since both she and Linda were tall and thin, I felt that this was an exaggeration.

"Don't tell me that Linda goes in for jogging, too?" I asked.

"Sure. She says it wakes her up after only having a few hours' sleep. No weights, though."

"I should hope not indeed," I said. "Where do you jog?"

"Sometimes along the promenade; weekends I go across the bridge."

"You must be very fit," I said enviously.

"Yes, well," she replied, taking her headband off and shaking out her short dark hair. "I work out at the gym as well, sometimes in the evenings, but mostly lunchtimes—it stops me from eating lunch!"

"Where's the gym?" I asked.

"It's at the college." Anna teaches Art History at one of the New York City colleges. "Which reminds me, I'm seeing a student at ten-thirty. I'd better take a shower. Are you coming in this morning? What do you plan to do?"

"If I get a move on, can I come in with you? I don't know if I can remember how to manage the subway on my own."

"Sure," she replied, and added, "I don't have to ask, do I? Bloomingdale's?"

Linda and Anna always tease me about the fact that when I'm abroad, I prefer wandering around department stores and supermarkets rather than improving my mind in museums and art galleries. But I maintain that all museums look alike, whichever country you're in, whereas there's no better way of getting the flavor of a country than in its shops.

"Yes." I laughed. "Bloomingdale's first, but I *do* want to go to the Frick—it's one of my very favorite places anywhere."

Walking through Brooklyn Heights on our way to Borough station, I reveled in the marvelously complex mixture of the familiar and the strange that I find in America: the handsome brownstone houses; the flower beds filled with busy lizzies; the locust trees that line the streets, dropping their strange fruit that looks like cocoa pods; the mailboxes that could be mistaken for litter bins; police with guns on their hips; chubby fire hydrants that look like examples of the cartoonist's art; elegant fire escapes with wonderful decorative ironwork. I seemed to see quite ordinary, everyday things with a fresh eye.

The subway train was shiny and metallic, and the carriages were spotless. "Goodness," I said, "no graffiti and look how clean! You should see London Transport!"

I spent a couple of wonderful, exhausting days in New York, marveling at the beauty of the city, walking in the evenings with Anna along the promenade, gazing at the breathtaking view of the Manhattan skyline across the water.

"It's going to be very hard to get down to work at Wilmot," I said as we sat in Chang's on my last evening, eating Hung Shao chicken and Hot Shredded Beef with Sour Plum Sauce. "I've had a simply wonderful time, and I can't thank you enough."

"It's nice to share New York with such an enthusiast." She smiled. "Here, have some of this tofu thing; it's really good."

"And," I continued, "it really is kind of you to drive me up to Wilmot tomorrow. It's an awfully long drive for you, there and back."

"I do it all the time," Anna said. "I do a lot of research at the Whittier Collection. They have one of the finest collections of early Italian paintings outside of the major galleries, you know."

"Is that part of the college?" I asked.

"No, it's housed in the old Whittier Mansion, just off the campus. Gorgeous place—you'll love it. So I drive back and forth several times a month, and I don't always stay over. Outside the rush hour I can do it in ninety minutes, portal to portal, as they say."

"What time should we leave tomorrow?"

"Well, since it's Sunday, how would you like to walk across the bridge with me first?"

"Across Brooklyn Bridge?" I asked in some alarm, thinking of the mad welter of cars and taxi-cabs that rushed endlessly across it. "Isn't it rather dangerous?"

Anna laughed. "Just wait and see."

It was a beautiful morning in early September, and the sun hadn't yet burned the moisture out of the air as Anna led me up to the pedestrian level of the bridge. The cars were down below, but up here, where the wooden planking under our feet was divided into lanes for pedestrians and cyclists, it was quite free from noise and exhaust fumes. Down below and stretching on either side was the blue water of the East River, opening out into the Upper Bay with Governors Island to the left and beyond that, just discernible in the distance, the Statue of Liberty. It was a wonderful feeling to be walking level with the skyscrapers, with the sparkling water below and the great arching struts of the bridge etched against the blue sky. Around us New Yorkers were jogging, cycling, or just out for a Sunday stroll, all apparently at peace with the world and each other.

"So much for the violent New York one is always reading about," I said as we were overtaken by a family of mother, father, and two children on bicycles, who all smilingly thanked us as we stood to one side to let them pass.

Anna laughed. "I guess there's violence just about everywhere if you care to look for it."

As we drove in the strange Sunday quiet of lower Manhattan, along Canal Street to the Holland Tunnel, Anna reverted to her earlier conversation about Linda.

"I'm glad she'll have you with her for a while," she said. "It'll make her relax a little, take a little time out to do other things besides work."

"As long as she doesn't expect me to go jogging with her," I said. "Does she have many friends at Wilmot?"

Anna paused as if considering the question.

"Yes, in a way. A lot of friends, sure, but none of them close. You know how she is."

It was true. I had known Linda for over fifteen years. We had first met when she was in England doing research for her doctorate on Mrs. Gaskell and had written to ask if we could meet to discuss a paper I'd published on *North and South*. We'd immediately taken to each other and she always spent a little time with us in the West Country whenever she was in England and was a great favorite with us all. Peter used to say that her enthusiasm and good humor always made him feel young again, and she certainly came into that rare category of life enhancers. And yet for all the warmth of her personality we've none of us got really close to Linda; there's always, in the final analysis, a barrier, something that says so far and no further. She hasn't married, though I know she lived for a while with an Englishman, David Hamble, a don at Wolfson, when she was in Oxford for a year. But she'd gone back to America when her research grant ran out and, as far as I knew, had never seen him again.

"Yes," I said, "I know how she is."

We drove on along Interstate 78, and I marveled as I always do at all the trees; I do believe that three quarters of America is covered by forest and woodland, but nobody ever tells you this, and it certainly comes as a delightful surprise.

"I just hope," I said, "that I won't add to Linda's burden; I shall have to rely on her to tell me how to go on. After all, *she* talked me into coming, and I must say I'm beginning to get cold feet about the whole thing!"

"You'll be great," Anna said as she nimbly overtook a vast truck with what seemed to be half a steam engine attached to its side. "They'll love you. Anyway, it won't matter what you *say*, the accent will get them."

This doubtful compliment did little to reassure me, and as we left New Jersey and drove on into Pennsylvania, I turned my attention to the billboards proclaiming the virtues of petrol, cola, and cars and advertisements for motels.

"Could you get me a tissue from my purse?" Anna asked. "It's on the backseat."

Anna's handbag was an enormous leather affair with a lot of compartments, all jammed full so that the clasp wouldn't shut.

"Goodness," I said, "I thought *my* bag was full!"

"Well," she said defensively, "you know how you always seem to get a lot of junk you just *have* to have with you!"

I scrabbled about in the bag and finally found a small packet of tissues and extracted one. "There you are." I tried to fasten the bag with little success. "*Does* it close?" I asked.

"Not really." Anna laughed. "I guess one of these days I'll lose something really vital. Well now, if you look to the left, you can see the college among the trees down there, by the river. What do you think? Are you going to like it?"

I looked at what I could see of the large buildings surrounded by trees with the glint of the river behind them; there appeared to be an awful *lot* of Wilmot College. It seemed pretty impressive, and I liked the look of it. What Wilmot thought of me I would doubtless find out quite soon.

2

Anna drew up in front of a white clapboard house with a handsome porch at the front.

"Here we are," she said. "Your home for the next four months, though I hope you'll spend an occasional weekend in New York. The ballet season starts in October."

She got out and started to unload the car. Wanting to help, I tried to lift a large bag, but I couldn't even move it. "What on earth is this?" I asked.

"Oh, *that*," said Anna. "That's Linda's computer. I had it repaired for her in New York."

She lifted it out with apparent ease, and I said enviously, "Goodness! I wish I was that strong!"

Anna laughed. "Come jogging, then!"

The door opened, and Linda came out to greet us. "Sheila! Isn't this *great*—you're here at last!"

We hugged each other, and I felt that coming all this way was worthwhile just to see Linda again. She always has this effect on people—as I said, a real life enhancer.

The two sisters embraced, and I thought how alike they were, both tall (though Linda was slimmer and more finely boned), both dark with clear gray eyes, and both lively and absolutely bursting with energy. I smiled at them fondly, basking in the warmth of their affection for each other, some of which spilled over onto me.

As we sat with our drinks ("Are you sure you wouldn't rather have tea?"), an enormous marmalade cat suddenly appeared, greeted Linda with a brief chirrup, ignored Anna and me, and leaped up on top of the television set, where he sat with his back to us and his tail hanging down in front of the screen.

"Oh, that's Tiger," Linda said. "I must apologize for his manners."

"Does he sit like that when the set is on?" I asked.

"That he does," she replied, laughing. "You sort of get used to watching a bisected picture after a while!"

Linda pushed a couple of dishes with nuts and olives in them and a wooden board with slices of cheese (I had forgotten that Americans eat cheese *before* a meal) towards me and said, "Before I forget, we're expected to go for cocktails with Rob and Martha Huron tomorrow; I think most of the people in the department will be there. That's throwing you in at the deep end!"

"Rob Huron," I said, "he's the head—I mean

26

chair—of the department, isn't he? Has he been here long?"

"About three years," Linda replied. "He came to us from Florida. He's a pleasant enough person, but—"

"He should never have been made chair," Anna broke in. "He has absolutely no control over Loring and O'Brien! What those two get away with!"

"Carl Loring," Linda explained, "our so-called drama specialist, and Nora O'Brien, who teaches American Literature."

"What do they get away with?" I asked curiously.

"Well, Loring," Linda said, "is a really awful man—lazy, sneaky, and generally *mean*. He tries to undermine the rest of us, is always whining to Rob about someone or something, urges his students to complain about teachers *he* doesn't like, wriggles out of anything that looks like *work*, never does anything extra for his students, and then there's the question of freshman comp—"

"What's that?" I asked.

"Freshman composition—the most hated course in any college," Linda said. "We all loathe it, but it has to be done, by everyone except Loring, who has somehow persuaded Rob that his talents would be better used in *administration*, if you please, on a great plan to reorganize the complete major and minor programs of the department. Thank God Loring is totally idle and obviously has no intention of ever completing the project or we'd all be working eight days a week and in a state of total chaos."

Anna spit out an olive stone.

"The man is vile," she said. "Look at the way he got that research funding Dave should have had last year. Off he went to Ontario for three months, with not a single thing to show at the end of it! As far as I can see, all he did was go up for the Shakespeare season because his boyfriend was acting there!"

"We don't know that!" Linda protested. "He's supposed to be giving a paper on the Ontario theater at the Cambridge conference next spring."

"Like he did last year, I suppose," Anna said scornfully.

"Yes, well, that was pretty peculiar." Linda turned to me. "It lasted just ten minutes, would you believe, and was the most disgusting nonsense you've ever heard, but being Loring, he got away with it."

"He sounds uniquely horrible," I said.

"As a matter of fact, he isn't," Anna said.

"Oh?"

"Unique, that is," Anna replied. "He has a brother, Max, who's almost as unbearable as he is."

"Goodness! And is his brother at Wilmot, too?" I asked.

"Thank God, no," Anna said. "But he's still too

near for comfort. He's head of research at the Whittier Collection—early Italian expert, so I come across him a lot."

"What form does *his* horribleness take?" I asked. "Is he lazy, too?"

"No," she replied, "even his worst enemy—and there must be quite a competition for *that* particular title—couldn't call him lazy. No, he's a smug, supercilious bastard, knows everything—in his own field and everyone else's. Like his nasty little brother, he's picky, too; he can't wait to find fault with things. If you had the most exquisite oriental vase ever created, he wouldn't admire its beauty; he'd be too busy looking for a flaw in the glaze!"

"Do the brothers get on?" I asked.

Linda laughed. "Do jackals in the same pack get on?" she said. "They loathe each other but gang up on the rest of society."

"I think," I said, "I will try to avoid them both as much as possible." I took another slice of cheese to fortify myself and went on, "So what about the O'Brien woman?"

"Oh, *her*," Linda said. "A bad case of power madness. Has to have a finger in every pie. Rob, of course, is only too glad to have someone who'll do things, but she's very selective—only wants to do things that'll advance her own prospects."

"Or those of her nasty little protégé," Anna broke in. "The unspeakable Rick!"

"Who is he?" I asked.

"Her cousin Rick Johnson," Linda said. "He's in the department, too. She got him the job, of course. There's no way anyone would employ *him* without some sort of pull being used!"

"What does he do?" I inquired.

"Teaches film," Linda said.

"Film!" I exclaimed. "He *teaches* film! How extraordinary!"

They both looked mildly surprised at my amazement.

"Yes," Linda said. "Here, let me freshen your drink."

She poured a large amount of gin into my glass and added a very small amount of tonic. I didn't protest because I felt I needed all the help I could get in this strange land where the movies were considered a subject suitable for a university syllabus.

"Goodness," I said, "didn't my generation miss out? There we were slogging away at Beowulf and Milton, and all the time we could have been writing essays on the comedic timing of Mae West or a comparison of the eye contact techniques of Bette Davis, Joan Crawford, and Barbara Stanwyck! So is this Rick person no good?"

"Dumb," Linda said vehemently, "and then some. But perfectly sure that he's God's gift to academe. A real slimeball!"

"Hey!" Anna broke in. "Give Sheila a break.

She'll think all of Wilmot's vile and be off on the next plane!"

Linda's face softened, and she said, "Oh, no, most of the people in the department are really nice—my friend Sara Heisick, for example. She's a medievalist—Chaucer mostly—and Dave Hunter, he's eighteenth-century studies. And then there's Ted Stern, who's a darling. He's retired, really, but he still teaches a few courses on modern literature, and his wife, Susan, is one of the nicest people I know. You'll love her."

I began to feel quite dizzy with all this information. Dizzy and rather apprehensive. I have never held a formal academic post or been part of an organization; I really didn't know how much of what they had described was normal departmental infighting, or if Wilmot was particularly cursed with tiresome and difficult people. I rather suspected the former, especially since both Linda and her sister appeared to bring equal zest and enthusiasm to their condemnations as to their praise. What I mostly felt, though, was a sort of despair at ever sorting out who was who among the staff, let alone the students.

"What about the students?" I asked Linda apprehensively. "The two who are writing master's theses; they'll be the ones I'll have most to do with, I suppose. What are they like?"

Linda's face lit up. "Oh, you'll really love them,"

she said. "Well, Sam, at any rate, and Gina is sweet, rather shy but very bright."

"Sam?" I asked. "I thought they were both females."

"Samantha Broderick," Linda said, "always known as Sam, is a mature student. She's working for her master's; her thesis is on Dickens's treatment of women."

"Is she a very fierce feminist?" I asked nervously. I never know what to say to declared feminists, since I often feel I have more in common with my mother's generation than with the brave new world of today, and (reprehensibly perhaps) dislike any sort of confrontation. "I suppose we're just born doormats," my friend Rosemary says resignedly, and I fear she may be right.

"I don't think you need to be nervous of Sam." Linda laughed. "She's an original, you'll love her. She's been married and is now divorced and living with a man who owns quite a large farm a few miles into Bucks County. The attraction is not so much the man himself as the fact that he owns all these lovely acres where Sam's two horses can roam free, not to mention her two dogs, her cat, and her Nubian goat."

"No!" I exclaimed. "How *marvelous!*"

"I told you," Linda said. "Twin souls."

"And what about the other one?" I asked.

"Gina. Gina Monticello. She's doing her thesis on Fanny Trollope's American journeys. So you see they're neither of them working exactly in your field, but what I want is for you to expand their perception of the period: background stuff, society, class—especially class. Americans are hopelessly ignorant of the nuances of the English class system, and it's so important in nineteenth-century English literature!"

"Well, I daresay I could do *that*," I said.

"And another thing I want you to do," Linda went on, "is to read aloud to my class—Dickens, George Eliot, the Brontës—just so that they can get a feeling of how the novels sound with an English accent."

"Oh, dear," I exclaimed, "I haven't read aloud since Michael was a small child."

"Well, there you are, then," Linda said.

"Yes, well," I replied doubtfully, "but that was *Winnie-the-Pooh* and books on dinosaurs."

After supper Anna disappeared to her room to go over some notes for a class she had the next day, while Linda and I washed up.

"I guess I'm the only person I know who doesn't have a dishwasher," Linda said, "but somehow I've never really got the hang of them."

"Anyway," I said, looking round her kitchen, "it wouldn't seem right to have one here."

The kitchen had wood-paneled walls, and the work tops were also wood with tiles set into them. The wide windowsills were crowded with pot plants and dishes of ripening tomatoes and peppers. There was a large wooden table and chairs and a colorful rug on the tiled floor.

"It really is gorgeous," I said, running my hand over one of the surfaces.

"Wood's cheap here," Linda said. "There's a lot of it all around."

"I suppose that's why everyone has those beautiful polished wood floors and staircases, though I do find *those* rather dangerous—no stair carpet."

"Wait till you see Sara's house," Linda said. "It's an old mill, and her husband—he's an architect— has done a wonderful job of remodeling it. He's done most of the work himself."

I wiped a large pasta dish carefully with a tea towel Linda must have brought back from England since it depicted Salisbury Cathedral.

"I know it sounds silly," I said, "but I really am rather nervous about all this. I've led such a narrow life since Peter died—you know, just living quietly in Taviscombe or making little forays to Oxford for research or London for the occasional theater. The thought of meeting all these new people does rather terrify me."

"You'll be fine," Linda said. "People like you, because you're interested in them."

"Nosy, friends would say." I laughed. "How about these awful people in your department? Will they hate me?"

"Oh, no," she replied. "You're not a threat to them, you see. No, as a visiting expert—"

"Ha!"

"Well, you are from England and you have published quite a bit in your field, certainly a lot more than most of *them* have, so they'll want to impress you. Just wait and see."

Anna had already left for New York when I got up the next morning, and Linda was nowhere to be seen, so I assumed she was out somewhere jogging. The kitchen was flooded with early-morning sun as I sat at the table drinking coffee and trying to get myself into the right frame of mind to face what would undoubtedly be a difficult day.

Linda burst into the room glowing with health and that sort of righteousness that comes from having just undergone demanding physical exercise while others are in bed.

"I haven't got a class until eleven," she said, "so just as soon as I'm showered and changed, I'm going to take you to breakfast at the Blue Moon Diner."

We drove through streets lined with those timeless American houses that don't seem to have changed in style for over a hundred years: white clapboard, front porch, back porch. Only the size and the occasional architectural flourish differentiated them. We passed several white churches, handsome and classical in design, and a cemetery, unfenced, with gravestones right down to the pavement—the sidewalk. Downtown Allenbrook looked strangely familiar and I couldn't think why until I realized that it was typical small-town America and I'd seen it—or rather, towns like it—many, many times in films or on television. The shops were small and mostly gathered in one main street.

"Here we are," Linda said, drawing up in front of a café. I followed her inside and we sat in a booth at a plastic-topped table with ketchup bottles and the waitress came and said, "How'd ya want your eggs?" and Linda said "Sunny side up," just like an old John Garfield movie.

"A few members of the faculty have breakfast here," Linda said. "Men, mostly; the women are all on diets or health kicks. Actually, that's Dave Hunter in the corner there. I'll introduce you when we've finished."

I glanced curiously in the direction she had indicated and saw a fair-haired man, in his early forties with heavy horn-rimmed glasses, maneuvering a portion of hash brown into his mouth while absorbed in what appeared to be a learned journal.

"Eighteenth-century studies," Linda said, following my gaze. "Very nice."

When we had finished our enormous breakfasts ("Oh, God, the calories in gorgeous fried eggs!" sighed Linda), we approached Dave Hunter, and Linda said, "Hi!"

He looked up quickly at the sound of her voice, and his face lit up with a smile.

"Hi," he said, rising as best he could in the narrow confines of his booth.

"Don't get up," Linda said. "We just wanted to say hello. This is Sheila, Sheila Malory, who's joining us this semester."

We shook hands, and Dave Hunter said, "I've heard a lot about you from Linda. And of course, I've read your books. It was your study of Charlotte M. Yonge that first introduced me to *The Daisy Chain*, for which I will be forever in your debt."

I gave what I hoped was a deprecating smile and said how happy I was to be at Wilmot. "A bit nervous, though," I added. "It all sounds rather formidable."

"Oh, we're a weird bunch," he said, "some of us weirder than others. But I'm sure everyone will be delighted to see you. Not just because you're *you* if you see what I mean, but because we're all so inward-looking, so involved with each other in the department, that a new face will be very welcome. It will give everyone something else to talk about besides freshman comp!"

He turned to Linda and said, "Which reminds me. Guess what Loring's done now?"

She groaned. "Don't tell me!"

"He's pushing for some awful new system of grading. He says that peer review and peer workshops should form part of the fundamental basis of the general evaluation of student work. Furthermore," he went on with a certain grim relish, "he feels that the individual instructors, while having a fair amount of independence in what they do in the classroom, should all adhere to the guidelines he has laid down in the suggested syllabus—to be drawn up by him, of course."

"Oh, God," Linda said, "I can't bear it! He seems to think he's God! What does Rob say?"

"That it's a very, *very* interesting idea," Dave said.

"I might have known that our beloved chair would be no use. Honestly, Dave, something's got to be done to stop Loring in his tracks."

Dave Hunter smiled affectionately at her vehemence. "Well, you can count me in for sure. You know that. We must rally the troops."

"Well, there's you and me and Sara and Ted. Do you think that O'Brien will be so upset at Loring's empire building that she'll come in with us and bring the unspeakable Rick with her?"

"Maybe. But don't forget, she might need Loring's backing for that highly expensive American lit conference she wants to impose on us."

"Hell, yes."

Linda suddenly recollected my presence. "Sorry, Sheila—all this politicking must be very boring for you."

"On the contrary," I said, "it's fascinating, like

something out of a novel about academic life! Anyway, if I'm going to be here for several months, I really ought to know what's going on in the department. I only wish I had a vote, or however it is you decide these things, so that I could help."

"The wretched thing is," Linda said bitterly, "that not only will we have to fight Loring's rotten plan, but we'll have to spend endless extra hours in tedious committee meetings. Anyway, we'd better be going. I want to show Sheila around before my first class. See you, Dave."

As we went back to the car she said, "Dave really is a nice guy, always cheerful and helpful. I don't know what I'd do if I didn't have him to sound off to! Poor Dave—his wife died in an automobile accident two years ago and left him with two small children. His mother's moved in with him, and they cope, but he must miss Elaine terribly."

But, I thought, as Linda drove out of the main street and down towards the river and the campus, it seemed to me that he was beginning to get over his loss. Certainly, the way that he looked at Linda indicated to me, if not to her, that he felt for her considerably more than the respect and esteem that might be inspired by a mere colleague. I looked forward to trying out my theory on Anna.

3

Wilmot is one of those small, private, rather prestigious colleges that are to be found in eastern America. Originally specializing in the sciences, because of the proximity of the great Pennsylvania steelworks, it now has quite a flourishing humanities division.

We drove through the center of town and across a handsome suspension bridge over the Allen River and there, along the banks of the river, were these imposing Victorian mansions.

"Built, of course," Linda explained, "by the great steel barons at the turn of the century, trying to rival those enormous houses that wealthy New Yorkers built on the banks of the Hudson, I guess. Some of them house the various departments; some are fraternity and sorority houses."

"Goodness, yes," I exclaimed. "Sigma Chi and all that—*just* like all those college movies!"

We passed an imposing building constructed on classical lines with a great many pillars and architraves, which Linda told me was the library, and (looking sadly out of place in all this architectural splendor) a modern, functional block, which was the administration center.

Linda drew up outside a large Gothic edifice covered with creeper that was just turning color and slid triumphantly into the one remaining parking space.

"Here we are," she said. "This is Brook Hall, where the English Department is."

Inside, to my surprise (since I had imagined dark gloomy paneling to match the exterior), everything was bright and airy with lots of glass and light wood. Linda's office was a large room, lined with bookshelves, with (to me at least) several unusual features.

"Goodness!" I said. "You've got a coffee machine, a refrigerator, *and* a microwave! Talk about civilization!"

"Sure, and look—I've rearranged things so that I can reach them all without moving from my desk! Dump some of those papers on the floor, and sit down."

I added a pile of papers from one of the chairs to a larger pile on the floor, sat down, and looked about me. The room was crammed with books, files, toppling piles of journals, and a large computer enthroned like a monarch on the desk. My eyes wandered around the bookshelves and spotted, with satisfaction, several of my own works.

Linda was sorting through some letters, ripping open envelopes and tossing the contents to one side to join the general confusion on her desk. She gave a cry of triumph. "Great! That article I need for the *Review* has come at last! It should have gone to the printer last week. . . ."

In addition to all her other activities, Linda is the assistant editor of the *Wilmot Literary Review*. The editor is the chair of the English Department ("a very, very honorary position," Linda says bitterly), and although she is forever threatening to give it up, it remains her cherished nursling and takes up any spare time she may have.

"Now all I need," she said, tossing the article into a folder labeled LATE LATE LATE, "is that review from Ross Morgan. *He's* on my blacklist from now on. Such a pity, really—"

"He seemed such a *nice* young man!" I finished the sentence for her; it's a favorite phrase and has become one of the many jokes we have accumulated over the years.

"Honestly, Linda," I expostulated, "*how* many years have you been editing this thing? I'd have thought you'd have learnt by now, there are no nice young reviewers. Speaking as a reviewer myself, I can tell you we're an unreliable lot, always putting off until tomorrow what should have been done last week."

There was a tap at the door, and a young woman came in. She was tall with fair, curly hair and a cheerful suntanned face enlivened by particularly brilliant blue eyes.

"Hi! Am I too early?"

Linda looked up. "No, that's fine. Sheila, this is my good friend Sara, Sara Heisick, our medievalist, also very sound on the unspeakableness of the Loring creature and the uselessness of Rob Huron. She's going to show you around and look after you until lunchtime, when I'm free. Okay?"

Sara gave me an exhaustive tour of the campus. We peered into the various classrooms, did a quick whiz round the library ("I'll bring you back for a closer look when our librarian, Liz Jenkins, is here"), had a nice browse in the college bookshop (which also sold T-shirts, sweaters, baseball caps, and—amazingly—children's bibs, all emblazoned with the Wilmot name and logo), and drove along the river to look at the fraternity and sorority houses.

"What's that very handsome building there?" I asked, pointing to a large mansion in the classical style that stood a little way back from the river on a slight eminence.

"That's the Whittier Institute," Sara replied. "It's not part of the college, just adjacent. As you can see, this used to be a very exclusive estate of mansions that the college bought up one by one to extend its original campus. But the old Whittier House was left by Henry Whittier—he was the steel magnate, I guess you know—in trust to

house his art collection. So it sits up there surrounded by what are now Wilmot administrative
buildings, but pretty aloof in every sort of way!"

The first couple of days passed in a confused blur
of impressions of people and places, but gradually
I began to find my way about the college and even
to recognize some of the people who greeted me.
I gave my first classes, and they seemed to go
down well; at least the students listened atten-
tively, though that might have been just good
manners (they were all very courteous) except that
they *did* ask a lot of quite pertinent questions, so
I was reasonably encouraged.

At Rob Huron's party I had met the rest of the
English Department. Apart from Sara Heisick and
Dave Hunter, both of whom greeted me like an
old friend, I also took an immediate liking to Ted
Stern (a marvelous little Thurberlike man with a
refreshingly sardonic sense of humor) and his
wife, Susan (large and comfortable, with a cozy
manner and a sweet smile, which I suspected
masked an incisive mind and sound common
sense). He was partly retired but still taught a few
classes in modern literature; she worked several
days a week in the library.

Sara introduced me to Nora O'Brien, one of
those small, formidable women, neat-looking and
full of energy, who always make me feel like some
slow-moving plesiosaur. She looked very Irish,

with flaming red hair and had, I was sure, a fierce temper to go with it. However, she greeted me in a friendly fashion, questioned me briskly about my knowledge of modern American literature, refrained from commenting on the lacunae revealed, and said that she would be interested to hear my views on the early women's suffrage movement in Britain. While I was still recovering from that, she introduced her cousin Rick Johnson, who had been hovering at her elbow throughout the conversation, and left us to confront each other.

I eyed him nervously. "So you teach film," I said, adding inadequately, "How interesting."

Taking this feeble comment for encouragement, he launched into a long disquisition on the importance of the moving image in interpersonal communication, or some such thing; after the first few minutes I was hopelessly lost in a wilderness of jargon and could only smile in what I hoped was an encouraging manner and interject, "Really!" or, "Goodness!" at intervals. My interlocutor appeared to be quite happy with this response and would, I imagine, have continued in full flow for the rest of the evening had not Rob Huron, who had greeted me briefly and formally as I arrived, come up and said that he wanted to have a really good talk about the theory of the teaching of writing in British universities.

I regarded the chair of the English Department

with some alarm, having no idea what such a theory might be and, indeed, not at all sure that anyone had ever formulated one. Fortunately, like Rick Johnson, he didn't really require anything from me but a seemingly attentive ear while he expounded his own theories. He was a tall, heavily built man, almost completely bald, with a weak mouth and a flaccid handshake. I decided that I didn't particularly care for him and could see why Linda and Sara were so scornful of his ability to control the worst excesses of the Lorings and O'Briens of his department.

I collected my wandering thoughts and tried to pay attention.

"If language is the medium through which we motivate and negotiate actions, then through language we construct and understand our world. Writing, then, is the means by which we understand and control *language*. . . ."

My thoughts drifted away again, and my eyes strayed round the room. A man had just come in. He was tall and thin with fine, regular features, delicately molded, indeed a genuine classical profile, with brown, curly hair and the most beautiful hands. He moved like a dancer, lithely and with grace. I wondered who he was. Linda had never mentioned anyone as stunning as this!

Rob Huron was asking a question. ". . . don't you agree?"

"Oh," I said hastily. "Most certainly I do. Absolutely."

I willed Linda to come and rescue me, and like an answer to prayer, she came up and said that the vice-provost would like a few words and took me away.

Remembering just in time to say pro-vost, I murmured a few civilities, and then Linda led me in the direction of the drink. Eschewing a glass of dark brown sweet sherry, which is what Mrs. Huron (large and upholstered in navy and white-patterned chiffon) seemed to think "all you British" liked to drink, I gratefully accepted a large vodka and tonic and drew Linda to one side.

"Who is that fabulous-looking man?"

"Fabulous? Where?"

I nodded in the direction of the newcomer.

"Him?" Linda said. "Oh, that's Loring."

I gazed at her in astonishment. "You never said he looked like a Greek god!" I said.

"*He* thinks he looks like a Greek god," Linda said sourly. "Handsome is as handsome does, and believe you me . . ."

She took a large gulp of her scotch and scowled over the rim of her glass at the subject of our conversation. As if he had caught her eye, Loring came towards us and, extending his hand to me, said, "I'm Carl Loring. You must be Sheila Malory. *Welcome* to Wilmot."

In some confusion I shook his hand and said, "Thank you. It's lovely to be here."

"I had hoped to see you before, to welcome you to the department, but I had to go to New York for a few days—the premiere of the new *Cherry Orchard, quite* the most important version since Komisayevsky's *seminal* production in the twenties, I'm sure you agree."

"Of course," I said, keenly aware of Linda seething beside me, "you teach drama, don't you?"

He gave me what he probably imagined was a boyish smile and said, "When I can *snatch* time from all the administrative chores that we poor academics are burdened with."

"The students all seem very enthusiastic," I said, "at least the ones I've met so far."

He smiled patronizingly at me and said, "Communication, discussion, *feedback*: that is what teaching is really about, don't you think? I only *wish* I could find more time for informal group sessions with the students, but what with departmental matters—there is so much that needs urgent reorganization"—here he shot a spiteful look at Linda—"and, of course, I have a *crushing* teaching load, and with research and writing— right this minute I have a publisher crying out for the update of my Stanislavsky bibliography. Well, you can see how *thinly* one has to spread oneself!"

"Oh, absolutely," I said. "Do you manage to get over to England sometimes?"

"I've been asked to give a few workshops for the RSC at Stratford and at the National," he said. I could see what Linda and Anna meant about his "preening." "And of course, I have a *great* many dear friends in the English theater. London is a second home to me. *Almost* the most civilized place in the world, don't you feel?"

"Actually, I rather loathe London nowadays," I said, "and I only go up there when I have to."

He gave me a pitying smile. "Ah, you live in the *provinces.* How *interesting.*"

"I live in Taviscombe, which is a small seaside town in the West Country," I said formally.

"Sheila is a great friend of Will Maxwell." Linda dropped the name neatly into the conversation. "You know, the dramatist. And of Oliver Stevens, the film and television director who won that Emmy award last year. They live in Taviscombe, too."

Carl Loring gave me a tight little smile and said, "And of course, there is *your* work, too—quite a little intellectual community!"

"You could say that," I replied.

He smiled again. "Well, now," he said, "if you have any problems here at Wilmot, don't hesitate to come to me. My door is always open, and however busy I am, I can always find time to lend a helping hand!"

As if to emphasize this fact he stretched out one of his exquisite hands towards me. For a moment I thought that it was some sort of dramatic gesture. Then, realizing that he was bringing, as it were, the audience to an end, I shook the proffered hand and he turned away.

Linda barely waited until he was out of earshot before she exploded. "Ha! Welcome to Wilmot! Any little problems! Jesus H. Christ, that man is a total, unmitigated *creep*! Who does he think he is? God? It isn't even as if he's assistant chair— that's Dave, by the way—I mean, goddammit, he's only been here five minutes—"

To distract her, I said, "Who is that marvelous girl who's just come in?"

She looked towards the door, where two young women were standing. One, the smaller of the two, with light brown hair, was dressed in a full-skirted cotton frock in a curiously old-fashioned style that made her look mouselike and dowdy.

Mind you, almost anyone would have looked dowdy next to the girl who stood beside her. She was tall and slim, with short, very blond hair. The cream suit, which set off her elegant suntan to perfection, was beautifully cut and obviously very expensive, as were her matching cream shoes with immensely high heels. Her long golden brown fingers were tipped with scarlet and embellished with a large number of what were obviously real diamonds. She looked so fantastic that one couldn't think of her as another woman, but only as some glamorous creature who had stepped out of the pages of a fashion magazine, someone to be admired as a work of art.

Linda's scowl vanished, and she smiled happily. "Oh, that's Sam," she said. "And Gina Monticello is the other one."

There was no need to ask which was which.

"Come on," she said. "I'll introduce you."

Samantha Broderick held out a slim hand, the wrist enclosed by a heavy gold bracelet, and said, "Hi, I'm really glad to meet you and *really* looking forward to our conferences together."

The voice was a shock. It was loud and rather strident with an accent that I, unused to such nuances, couldn't identify.

"I love England and everything English," she went on enthusiastically. "I drink Earl Grey tea and love Tiptree's strawberry jam—they have it at Bloomingdale's, you know—and there's that wonderful English *soap,* and I always make Hal—he's my partner—buy English shoes and those great Burberry raincoats!"

"And Dickens, too?" I asked, smiling.

"Oh, well, sure. Victorian *society,* that really was something. The levels of *acceptance,* the ambivalence of standards—when I think of the position of nineteenth-century women I could actually throw up!" All this with a dazzling smile and a warmth that seemed to bind one into a cozy intimacy, so that it seemed that we had been old friends for years. I could see that Hal (or any other man for that matter) wouldn't stand a chance.

"And this," said Linda, "is Gina."

It said a lot for Sam's friendly naturalness as well as Gina's good nature that the latter seemed not at all offended at being produced almost as an afterthought.

"Hello, Gina," I said. "I'm so pleased you're doing some work on Fanny Trollope. She is a great favorite of mine. A wonderful woman and an extraordinary mother!"

Gina gave a shy little smile. "I've always been interested in Victorian women travelers, missionaries and people like that." Her voice was very soft and quiet so that I had to strain to hear what she was saying.

"As a mother," I said, "I've always been full of admiration about how she *coped* with that awful husband and those children in what must have been a dreadful situation. Not to mention keeping the family going simply by her writing!"

"Of course," Gina said, "the position of the writer, whether male or female, in the nineteenth century was so different, their influence—well into this century, actually—was pretty great. . . ."

I was delighted with both my students and told Linda so when we finally managed to extricate ourselves from the Hurons' party and had settled down cozily in her kitchen.

"They're a strange contrast," she said, putting

an enormous pizza into the microwave. "This is only frozen, but I've put lots of extra mozzarella on it. No, you wouldn't think they had anything in common—except English literature, of course—but they're good friends. And surprisingly, it's Gina who looks out for Sam and not the other way around."

"I *do* see what you mean about Loring," I said. "What a nauseating man—patronizing, slimy, and conceited! And the good looks somehow make it worse. I mean, you expect someone who looks like that to be, well, equally special in character, so it's almost like a blow in the face when he starts to speak! Does he really have that much power in the department?"

"He had poor Rebecca Long thrown out last year; she was an assistant professor and didn't have tenure."

"But how?" I asked.

"Oh, a sort of whispering campaign," Linda replied. "Complaints to the chair and to the dean from some of the students. He has his followers you know, all well organized. And at meetings he'd always manage to make her seem inefficient or unreasonable, as if she didn't fit in. Little things and all done very carefully so that it wasn't easy to say that he was behind it. But he was."

"Why did he want to get rid of her?" I asked.

Linda took the pizza out and divided it into two.

"Come on, let's eat."

She poured some wine, and we sat down.

"Loring hated Rebecca," she said, "because she gave a paper at a conference that argued against one of his books. It revealed his superficiality and lack of scholarship. Of course, his acolytes couldn't wait to tell him, and when he got to hear of it, that was the end of Rebecca! He was out to get her from then on."

"Goodness, how awful! What happened to her?"

"I don't know. She went to Washington, and I think she's teaching high school, one of those awful inner-city schools. Academic jobs are hard to come by just now, and Loring saw to it that word got around that she was 'unreliable.' "

I cut into my pizza and maneuvered the long, cheesy strands into my mouth.

"It's terrible," I said after a moment, "that he should have been able to do such a thing."

"The man is vile," Linda said, as if that explained everything.

She suddenly got to her feet and took an envelope that had been tacked onto her bulletin board. "I forgot," she said. "This came for you. It's an invitation to a concert at the Whittier Institute. I have one, too."

"How lovely," I said. "I'm longing to see that place. It looks like Xanadu all by itself out there."

"It is a gorgeous house, and the collection is fabulous, you'll love it. I'll ask Theo Portman to give you a tour after the concert; he's the curator and a good friend of Anna's. She'll be there, too, by the way. You'll like him a lot."

I wondered if Max Loring would be at the concert, since he worked at the institute. I was curious to see if he was as unspeakable as his brother.

4

Anna arrived quite early on the morning of the concert.

"I have some stuff to check in the research center, so it all fits in quite well," she said, unloading the usual collection of files, computer printouts, and general impedimenta from her car.

"Do you want breakfast?" Linda asked.

"What the hell, who wants to live forever?" Anna said. "Have you got any of those English muffins?"

We sat cozily round the kitchen table, eating muffins and waffles and drinking coffee.

"There's a sort of reception before the concert," Linda said. "Cocktails and stuff, which is why it's an invitation-only affair—just Wilmot people, mostly ones you know."

"And Loring's brother?" I asked.

"Oh, him, sure," Anna said. "Most of the research center staff will be there. Oh, and Walter Cleveland—he's always invited to things. He's the head of the U.S. division of Orlando, you know, the multinational petrochemical firm. They're based here in Allenbrook. They fund a lot of arts projects at the institute and at Wilmot."

"Modern industrialists are the merchant princes of the present day, twentieth-century Medicis, you might say," I reflected, "patrons of the arts—"

"I'll bet Machiavelli could pick up a few tips from their vice-presidents," Linda said, "about power and such."

"What is this Walter Cleveland like?" I asked.

"High-powered but nice—what you might call cultured, I suppose. He's at the opera a lot and the ballet, and he's bought some very expensive art for the company pension fund. Many, many millions of dollars. Very knowledgeable, they say, though of course, he does have advisers. Theo Portman thinks pretty highly of him."

"Well now," Linda said, "will you meet us in the common room, Anna, and we'll all come back here? Dress is formal at these things, so I'll have to come back and put a skirt on."

"How formal?" I asked in alarm, mentally reviewing my wardrobe.

"Oh, just ties and jackets for the men and skirts for the women. I think Theo really likes to feel he's having a sort of Victorian soiree, so we indulge him."

"Can I borrow an iron, please? My better dress is still a bit crumpled from the suitcase."

We assembled in Linda's sitting room, looking, I must say, rather good. Linda and Anna, tall and handsome, both elegant in silk suits, Linda's a rich plum red and Anna's a pale coffee color. And my little black dress, veteran of many Taviscombe social occasions, looked positively new on this side of the Atlantic.

I scrabbled in my bag for my invitation. "For one awful moment I thought I'd lost it," I said, "and I don't expect they'd let me in without it!"

"Well, as a matter of fact," Linda said, checking her own card, "they are a bit fussy about security, as you can imagine."

"Hell!" Anna exclaimed. "I can't find mine! I know I had it here somewhere."

Linda groaned. "That purse of yours," she said. "It's a miracle you can find *anything* in it ever! Here, let me look."

"Don't boss me, little sister," Anna said, keeping hold of the bag. "I know I had it right here, in the front compartment."

"That damned thing is stuffed so full you haven't been able to fasten it in years," Linda said in exasperation. "Do you know"—she turned to me—"at the last count, as well as the usual junk, I found six lipsticks, five congealed packs of fruit drops, three combs, a program for the Met's last season but one and a New York to Allenbrook bus schedule for 1986! And that was just on top. God knows what lurks on the bottom!"

Anna abandoned her cursory search and flicked the flap over the straining bag. "I guess it must have fallen out. I just hope it's Josh or Kurt at the door. They'll let me in."

A tall, heavily built man, a gun strapped to his side, beamed cheerfully at Anna as we entered the wide classical portico of the Whittier Mansion.

"Josh," she said, "I've lost my invitation. Can I come in?"

He wagged an admonitory finger at her. "Well, you know the rules, Dr. Kowolski. Nobody comes in here without one of those big white invitation cards, like your sister has, and your friend," he said, taking our cards from us. He gave a great wide grin and turned his head away from her. "But since I didn't see you go in, then I don't need no card, do I?"

"Thanks, Josh, you're a friend."

We went through a spacious hallway, full of oriental lacquer chests and cabinets, into a large room with an ornate plasterwork ceiling.

"Italian," Anna said, following my upward gaze. "Henry Whittier brought craftsmen over from Italy to do all the plasterwork and mosaics when the house was built in 1887."

The walls were crowded with magnificent pictures, here a Titian, there a Canaletto. I moved across the room to look at a superb Veronese.

"It is splendid, isn't it?" a voice at my elbow said. "They have a couple of Veronese allegories at the Frick, but I like to think that ours is even finer."

I turned to find a tall, dark man with a small, pointed beard. He held out his hand. "Theo Portman," he said. "I'm the curator and a friend of your friend Anna."

"Of course," I replied. "It was so kind of you to invite me this evening. This place is fantastic—well, it must be if this room is anything to go by!"

"If you can spare the time after the concert," he said, "I'd love to show you around."

Linda and Anna led me through several rooms and out into a sort of atrium, with pillars and a fine marble pavement. All round the walls stood great urns full of plants, mostly ferns and palms. The lush greenery looked cool and inviting on a hot evening, and at one end, the gentle fall of water from the fountain into a pool covered with water lilies added to the charm of the scene.

"Oh, this is lovely!" I exclaimed.

There were about thirty people gathered in the atrium. A lot of the staff of the English Department seemed to be there, and I exchanged greetings with most of them, though avoiding Loring, who was holding court beside the fountain.

"Where's Loring's brother?" I asked Linda. "I'm dying to see him."

She looked around. "Not here yet. I expect he's planning to make an entrance. Oh, there's Walter Cleveland. I'll introduce you."

She moved towards the door, where a man was standing by himself, quietly surveying the company. He was tall and distinguished-looking in a beautifully tailored gray suit and what seemed to be a Garrick Club tie. I don't know why I should have been surprised that he was black.

"Walter," Linda said, "this is my friend Sheila Malory, who's come over from England to teach in our department for a semester."

We shook hands, and I said how much I admired the Whittier Collection and its setting.

"Well," he said, smiling, "it's certainly nice of you to be so appreciative when I know that you have so many remarkable collections and many more beautiful houses than this. I love England. I like to get over there whenever I can." He laughed, a splendidly warm sound. "Certainly for Glyndebourne and I never miss Wimbledon! Where do you live?"

"Oh, a very small West Country town you wouldn't have heard of."

"Is it near Bath? I like to get there for the festival. Now *there's* a superb setting!"

As we chatted, I became more and more aware of the intellectual strength and shrewdness that lay beneath the veneer of charm and ease of manner. I imagined that in business he could be very ruthless, a real twentieth-century merchant prince with power, perhaps not quite over life and death, but very great nonetheless.

"If you are interested in American nineteenth-century architecture," Walter Cleveland said with a smile, "you might be interested in seeing our company's headquarters here in Allenbrook. Not, maybe, as fine as this"—he indicated our elegant surroundings with a wave of his hand—"but not atypical of the period and the genre. If you would like to have lunch one day, I'd be pleased to show you around. We have quite a few paintings and other works of art you might like to see."

I thanked him and said that I'd be delighted, reflecting that my friends in Taviscombe would be surprised at the apparent novelty value of an English visitor in high-powered business circles in America.

After we had all consumed several glasses of champagne (the funding of the Whittier Institute was apparently pretty sound) and eaten a quantity of what Michael calls bits of minced-up fish on toast, we all moved on into an elegant oval salon, its walls lined with French cabinets heavy with ormolu and hung with paintings by Watteau and Fragonard.

The music, however, was German—Beethoven quartets—and the performance (like everything else connected with the institute, it seemed) of a very high quality.

The concert lasted just over an hour, and afterwards, as we were all standing about in groups, chatting, Theo Portman came up and said, "Would you like to take the grand tour now?"

I turned to Linda and Anna and said, "Is that all right with you? Are you coming, too?"

"Sure," Linda said. "I can never see all this" — she waved her arms in an embracing gesture— "too often. How about you, Anna? Oh, I forgot, you've got to get back to New York."

"Tonight!" I exclaimed. "It'll be dreadfully late!"

Anna laughed. "I'm used to driving at night; it doesn't worry me. I wanted to be here this evening, but I've got a boring but important committee meeting tomorrow first thing, and I'd better not risk the morning rush hour!"

We followed Theo Portman out into the hall, and he led us through room after room of fine pictures, commenting as he went. "Henry Whittier was already a considerable collector when he built this house, so he had the architect design many of the rooms downstairs to display the pictures to their best advantage. We've changed very little in the way of arrangement since his death."

"When did he die?" I asked.

"In 1921, but his wife, who was much younger, lived until the 1950s, and it was she who really set up this whole institute—all the research side, especially. Isn't that a gorgeous Turner?" He broke off to gesture towards the far wall. "Stand over here and you'll find it's the best angle. . . .

I don't believe the Tate has a better example of his work."

Theo's tremendous pride in the collection and enthusiasm for it were justified and endearing.

"I'm particularly fond of these," he said as we stood in a long, beautifully lit room, filled with light and color from an incredible collection of French Impressionist paintings. "Mr. Whittier bought them as contemporary art when he was in Paris. I love to think of that. He bought them not as collector's pieces, but simply because he *liked* them!"

"That's nice," I agreed.

"Would you like to see upstairs? It's a fine house in its own right. Not old by British standards, of course, but very typical of the large mansions being built by the great industrialists of the day."

I love looking over houses, large or small, and this was a really remarkable one. Upstairs most of the twenty or so bedrooms were now divided up into offices and study rooms for the research center, but Theo Portman's office still had its original splendor.

"It was Mrs. Whittier's boudoir," he said, "and a bit feminine, though not quite as frilly and fussy as Mrs. Theodore Roosevelt's boudoir at Oyster Bay, Long Island. Have you seen that house yet? You really should. But I kept the Louis the Fifteenth furniture and that Greuze and that particularly fine Nattier—oh, and the Van Dyck, of course."

Hanging behind his desk was a portrait of a seventeenth-century gentleman who bore an extraordinary resemblance to Theo Portman himself, small, pointed beard and all.

Linda and I exclaimed delightedly, and he smiled with pleasure.

"My little joke," he said. "I couldn't resist it."

"It must have needed an enormous staff," I said, "to keep all this up."

"Indeed. Practically the whole of the top floor was servants' quarters. We keep the computers and so on up there. Would you like to have a look?"

We ascended a smaller and plainer staircase than the handsome, ornately carved one leading up from the great hall. The top floor was a warren of corridors, the labels on whose doors proclaimed them to be study and photocopying rooms or, more simply, "Administration." Theo Portman opened a few doors to reveal an impressive array of electronic equipment, which had Linda asking eager questions. She's a terrific computer enthusiast and actually seems to understand them and, I must admit, when I see her making an index, say, on her own machine, I do see the point of them and feel very much that I'm living in the Stone Age with my own cards-in-a-shoebox method!

"Oh, yes," Theo said, "there *is* something up here you might be interested to see."

We went down yet another corridor, and he opened a door into a large room, lined with shelves, which, in addition to the usual complement of computers, had walls laden with files.

"This," he said, "used to be the linen room. All those shelves used to hold linen. Smell the wood; it's all cedar, antimoth, you see. And this"—he unwound a sort of roller affair—"was how they stored those enormous damask tablecloths, so that they didn't crease."

"How gorgeous," I said, sniffing at the wood. "The cedar smell is still very strong. And what marvelous *quality* it all is and how beautifully made, everything just so and splendidly *planned!*"

"Oh, yes," Theo said, "a lot of thought went into the smallest detail." He moved to the far corner of the room towards what seemed like a couple of enormous chests.

"These are blanket chests, also lined with cedar, of course. You see, this looks like a drawer, but actually it swings out on a pivot just below waist level so you don't have to stoop to put things in."

He put his hand on one of the chests, pulled gently, and the side section swung out, revealing a deep box.

But the box wasn't empty. Lying inside it was the body of a man.

5

The man was neatly laid out in the great chest, as if in a coffin. There was a bullet hole in his head. For one extraordinary moment I thought I recognized him, but he was no one I had ever met.

"Oh, my God," Linda exclaimed, "it's Max Loring!"

I nerved myself to look again at the body and saw that the man in the chest did indeed look very like his brother, though he was smaller and of slighter build.

Theo, who still had his hand on the chest, swung it shut. He was very pale, and his hands were trembling as he fumbled with the box.

It seemed somehow awful to shut the body away like that, almost as if we were denying its existence. But I'm sure we all had a fleeting wish that it *could* be shut away forever.

For a moment nobody said anything. It seemed too big a happening to take in. Then Theo, with an obvious effort, pulled himself together and said, "I'm so sorry, Sheila. I wouldn't have had you see such a terrible thing for the world. Are you all right?"

"Yes, yes, I'm fine," I said shakily. "Linda?" I turned to her. "How about you?"

She shook her head as if to dismiss the sight that had distressed us all. "Yes," she said abruptly, "I'm all right."

"The police," Theo said suddenly. "I must call the police."

He moved towards the door, and we followed him. I cast a look around the room, such an ordinary room now that the body of Max Loring had been tidied away. So prosaic in the cold, fluorescent light, with the shelves full of files, the closed chests, and the dark blank window giving back our reflections. And, over everything, the faint, sweet smell of cedarwood.

Theo phoned the police from his office, while Linda and I sat silently like two obedient children waiting to be told what to do next. Suddenly I felt very tired. I looked at my watch and was surprised to see that it was only ten-thirty. It seemed as if an entire night had passed since the concert. Theo put down the telephone.

"I must go see who, if anybody, is left here," he said. "I'm afraid the police would like you both to stay until they've questioned us all. I'll have some coffee sent up—or would you like something stronger?"

"No," Linda said, "coffee's fine."

For a few moments after he had gone we sat in silence, possessed, it seemed, by a sort of lethargy. Then Linda got up and began to walk about the room.

"Max Loring," she said, "I can't believe it."

"I wonder if his brother's still here," I said. "It will be a terrible shock for him."

"Yes," Linda said, "it will. It's a terrible thing to lose a brother."

I remembered Dan, dead in Vietnam, and cursed my thoughtlessness.

"Do you think anyone will still be here?" I asked, more to change the subject than with any real wish to know.

"I guess a few may have hung on. There was some more wine and food set out for after the concert, I think."

After a while one of the institute's guards arrived with a tray of coffee and said that the police had arrived and Mr. Portman would be with us shortly.

We drank our coffee in silence; I think we were both still in that state of shock when simply speaking seems like too much of an effort.

"I'm sorry to have kept you." Theo was back in the room. "This is Lieutenant Landis of the Police Department, who wants to ask you a few questions."

The lieutenant was a big man, heavily built, with the sort of heaviness that comes from a large appetite and not enough exercise. He was middle-aged, and his long-jawed face had deep lines etched by the years from nose to mouth. His hair was thick and straight and gray, brushed back from a high forehead. He was wearing a navy blue suit and a lighter blue tie, slightly askew under a crumpled shirt collar. He looked tired, as if he'd already had a hard day.

"The lieutenant's going to use my office to interview people," Theo said, "so would you like to come with me, Sheila, while he has a word with Linda?"

We went into an adjoining office and sat on either side of a large desk.

"Were there many people left?" I asked Theo.

"Just a few," he replied. "The Hurons and Dave Hunter. Oh, and Nora O'Brien and Rick Johnson, a couple of others from the institute."

"What about Carl Loring?"

"No," Theo said, "he'd gone. He left right after the concert. The police are trying to get in touch with him now."

"It will be awful for you," I said, "having the police all over the place."

"And the media," said Theo gloomily. "We don't get many murders in Allenbrook, and the fact that the body was found in such, well, *bizarre* circumstances will bring the whole pack of them down on us. Not the sort of publicity the institute needs right now."

I looked at him inquiringly.

"Funding," he said, "as always."

"I thought you were quite well off with the Whittier millions," I said, "and don't you get something from the Orlando group?"

"Oh, sure. But as you said, this place has always taken a lot of upkeep, and every year it gets more difficult, what with heating and security and such—not to mention insurance. No, we were just on the verge of launching a new appeal statewide. This couldn't have come at a worse time. Trust Max Loring to screw things up as usual!"

Seeing my startled expression, he said, "Forget I said that! No, I expect you will have heard from Anna that he was a very tiresome man, not easy to work with—hell on committees." He gave a short, sardonic laugh. "It just seems like the last straw that he should have been killed in such a way that will make things difficult for the institute!"

The door opened, and a uniformed policeman put his head round. "The lieutenant'll see Mrs. Malory now."

As I followed him into Theo's office, Linda rose to go. "I'll see you downstairs when you've finished," she said. "In the main hall."

She went out, followed by the other policeman.

"Sit down, please." The lieutenant had a deep, pleasant voice. "There's coffee left if you'd like some."

"No, thank you," I replied. "I'm fine."

"You're sure? You must be kind of shook up." He drew the tray towards him. "I guess I'll have a cup."

He poured a cup of coffee, drank a little, then sat back and regarded me.

"You're British?"

"English," I said. "Yes, that's right."

"You'll think all the things you've heard about violence in the States are true," he said, "but I guess this kind of thing doesn't happen too often in Allenbrook. As a matter of fact"—he laughed—"*this* kind of thing—bodies of art experts in blanket chests—doesn't happen at all!"

I gave a reluctant smile, and he continued. "Have you been over here long?"

"Just a couple of weeks," I replied.

"And do you like it here?" His very blue eyes were fixed on me sharply, as if this were somehow an important question.

"Oh, yes," I said. "I love being at Wilmot. It's so different from anything I've ever done before."

"And what have you done before?" Again he seemed anxious to hear my answer.

"Oh," I replied, rather taken aback. This wasn't at all what I had expected. "I've led a very quiet life in a small country town."

He glanced down at a paper on the desk. "Some kind of visiting professor at Wilmot?" he asked.

I laughed. "Nothing as grand as that! I've written a few books on English literature, but I've never actually taught in a university at all."

"Is that so?" He reached forward to put his coffee cup back onto the tray. "A kind of amateur? Isn't that what you British like to call yourselves?"

"An amateur," I said rather formally, "in the strict sense of the word—a lover of English literature."

He nodded approvingly. "I like that," he said. "I'm a kind of lover of English literature myself."

He leaned back comfortably in Theo's chair and regarded me amiably. "Well, Shakespeare mostly," he said. "If you have Shakespeare, you have the best."

"I love Shakespeare," I said warmly, "as a person as well as a writer, if you know what I mean. He's so real. I can't imagine how there could be any doubt that he wrote the plays—not if you've ever been to Stratford and wandered about the Warwickshire countryside. Have you ever been to Stratford?"

"Not yet," he said. "But pretty soon, when I retire, I mean to go there and stand on that bridge—what's it called?"

"Clopton Bridge."

"Yes, that's right, Clopton Bridge, and see those old houses and the school, and the church where he's buried, and the river and that Forest of Arden—"

He broke off, and the words seemed to hang in

the air. I suddenly felt how extraordinary it was that a man had been killed and here I was, at eleven o'clock at night, talking about Shakespeare with an American detective.

As if he had caught my thoughts, Lieutenant Landis took out a notebook and assumed a more official expression. "Well, I guess I'd better get your statement down," he said.

He asked me about discovering the body and if I knew the deceased.

"No," I said, "I'd never seen him before. I've met his brother, of course, at Wilmot."

He closed his notebook. "You'll be around," he asked, "until the end of the semester, in case anything crops up and I need to see you again?"

"Yes," I replied, "I'm here for four months."

I got up to go, and to my surprise he rose, too, and held out his hand. "Thank you, Mrs. Malory. It was nice meeting with you. I hope you enjoy the rest of your stay."

We shook hands, and as he moved towards the door and opened it for me, he gave me a warm smile.

"Good-bye and thank you," he said.

I found myself smiling back, and indeed, I was still smiling as I made my way down the great staircase to find Linda waiting for me in the hall.

I hastily composed my face into a more suitable expression.

"Sorry to be so long, Linda," I said, "but we were chatting."

"Chatting?" She looked startled.

"About Shakespeare, mostly," I said.

"Shakespeare?" she echoed, looking at me with concern.

"No, really," I said. "He's a Shakespeare freak, as you would say. Longs to go to Stratford-on-Avon."

Linda shook her head. "Cultured policemen I can do without at this time of night."

She led the way out of the great house and down the drive to where the car was parked. There were still a few other cars, looking scattered and lonely as cars do when all their companions have gone, waiting for their owners.

"Who's still there?" I asked.

"Mostly institute people," Linda replied, "and the Hurons. I think Rob feels that as the senior Wilmot person here tonight he has to stay to the bitter end."

She smiled wryly. "Even at a time like this he's very conscious of his status."

By the time we got back home it was well past midnight, and perversely, I felt wide-awake. So, apparently, did Linda.

"Do you want some coffee or a real drink?" she asked.

"What I'd *really* like," I said, feeling stereotyped even as I spoke the words, "is a nice cup of tea."

Linda gave a little crack of laughter. "Of *course,* you would. And so, actually, would I."

"And," I suggested, "some cheese and biscuits, I mean, crackers."

We sat with our elbows on the kitchen table, mugs of comforting tea cradled in our hands.

"I just can't take it in," Linda said. "Did all that really happen or did we dream it?"

I had a sudden vivid picture of the face of the man lying in the blanket chest, a bullet hole in his head, and I shuddered.

"Yes," I said shakily, "it was real all right."

"Max Loring—God!" Linda cut herself another piece of cheese and pushed the board towards me. "He was a pretty loathsome creature, but— murder!"

"I wonder how long he'd been there?" I said. "He wasn't at the concert, was he?"

"I didn't see him," she replied, "so perhaps he'd been—you know—*there* quite a while. That makes it worse, somehow."

"You mean, all the time we were listening to that beautiful music he was already lying there, dead?"

I shuddered again, and Linda looked at me critically.

"You're bushed," she said. "Finish up your tea and go to bed."

"You too," I countered. "You look simply awful!"

Indeed, she did, her eyes enormous with exhaustion, the pallor of her face accentuated by the rich red of her jacket.

"I hope you don't even *think* of going out jogging tomorrow."

I got up stiffly from the table and went over to put my mug in the sink. "Thank goodness Anna went back to New York tonight. She'd have had practically no sleep at all if she'd had to leave at crack of dawn."

I thought I'd have a bad night, tossing and turning with the image of Max Loring's face floating before me, but to my surprise, I went out like a light and didn't wake until Linda materialized at my bedside with a mug of tea.

"I looked in earlier," she said, "but you were sleeping like a child."

"What time is it?" I struggled up on to one elbow and looked at my bedside clock. "Oh, no! Half past eight! I've got a tutorial—sorry, what do you call it? A *conference*—with Sam at nine!"

"It's okay," Linda said. "I called her and told her what had happened. I checked your schedule, and you can see her tomorrow at ten."

"Linda, you're an angel." I sat up, sipping my tea gratefully and trying to come to terms with the world again. "Good heavens," I said, taking in her tracksuit and trainers, "don't tell me you've been out already?"

"Sure. Did me the world of good. I don't need

much sleep. To be honest, it sort of blew the unpleasantness away a little."

"What did Sam say?" I asked. "About Max Loring. Did she know him at all?"

"Only as much as we all did, I guess. About enough to know that she didn't like him. Max was in and out of Wilmot quite a bit, actually, partly because of Carl and partly because he used to teach a course on fine arts before he was full-time at the institute, and he had a few friends here. Well, what pass for friends in Loring circles—toadies and hangers-on. You know the sort."

I finished my tea.

"Did Sam mind changing the tutorial?"

"No," Linda said, "I think she was kind of glad. Today's her big day, and she was pleased to have the extra time."

"Her big day?" I echoed.

"Sure, didn't I tell you? She's definitely going to marry Hal, and today's the day he's going to sign the prenuptial contract."

"Good heavens," I said. "How very eighteenth century!"

"Sam is a smart woman," Linda said. "She's been through all the hassle of a divorce with her first husband, and now she wants everything tied up and legal before she embarks on matrimony again. She's got a good lawyer. I gather Hal's finally agreed to six million."

"What!"

Linda smiled at my astonishment. "He's a rich man," she said. "You must have noticed all those diamonds."

"I thought he was a farmer," I said.

"Oh, the farm—and that's pretty big—is just a hobby. He lives there because that's where Sam wants to be—the animals, you know. But he has business interests all over."

"Good gracious!" I said. "All that, and she still wants to be a mature student!"

"Sam is a very serious woman," Linda said. "She cares a lot about literature, and she's determined to finish her master's thesis."

"I think she should do well," I said thoughtfully. "She's very conscientious and well organized in her work. It surprised me, actually. She looks immensely frivolous—all those high-fashion clothes—but when she's talking or writing about her own subject, she's very sound. More so, really, than Gina. Now I thought that she would be really *solid,* but somehow she doesn't seem to be bringing her mind to bear on what she should be doing. It isn't that she's not bright, she's very intelligent, but, I don't know, she isn't focusing her attention on her work."

"You think she's got something on her mind?" Linda asked.

"That's the feeling I get," I replied. "Of course I hardly know her, so I don't like to ask any personal questions—"

"Maybe I should speak to her," Linda said.

"Boyfriend trouble?" I asked.

"Not with Gina," Linda replied. "She doesn't care for men."

Tiger, who had come into the room, suddenly jumped onto my bed and began kneading the covers with his claws.

"No, Tiger," I said. "I'm getting up now."

He ignored me and came up onto the pillow, rubbing his head against my arm.

"Oh, Tiger!" I said weakly. "Well, perhaps five more minutes."

He curled up beside me, purring loudly, and Linda laughed.

"I'll leave you two," she said. "I'm going to have a shower. Have a rest; you've had a bad experience, after all. Take things easy this morning. You've got nothing scheduled until three-thirty."

I settled myself more comfortably and stroked Tiger's tawny head. "What about you?"

Linda groaned.

"Departmental committee meeting. Still"—she brightened up—"perhaps Loring will be so upset about his brother he won't show up!"

When Linda returned at midday to collect some books and to have what passes for lunch with her (an apple and a mug of herbal tea), I asked her if Carl Loring had been at the meeting.

"He sure was," she said. "Rob Huron made a little speech about how sorry we all were about

Max, and he sat there—well, I won't say he was actually *reveling* in it, but he certainly was pleased to be the center of attention. He had on that *smug* look I loathe so much. Goddammit, his brother was killed last night, and there he was—Honestly, Sheila, I went to that meeting prepared to feel sorry for the sleaze!"

She bit fiercely into her apple, and I said, "Perhaps he's one of those people who hide their real feelings."

Linda snorted. "Feelings! That creep has nothing you could describe as feelings! No, he obviously doesn't give a damn about Max's death, except to bask in whatever sympathy he can call up and use it as an excuse for getting his own way. Do you know he nearly got away with what he calls peer workshops for students to evaluate the feedback on their writing—can you believe the jargon!—because we all felt bad about really laying into him today. Fortunately Dave realized what the little toad was up to and put a stop to it, but it was a close thing!"

The next day, when she came for her conference, I regarded Sam with something like awe. She was looking marvelous in what looked like a Chanel original, and she appeared to have yet another diamond ring, larger and even more sparkling than the rest, on her engagement finger. She gave me a brilliant smile and handed me a large paper bag.

"Hi!" she said. "I baked you some bread, fresh this morning." Inside the bag was a golden brown, intricately plaited loaf.

"Oh, Sam, how kind. It smells heavenly. I can hardly resist eating it here and now!"

"I love to bake and I was up early this morning because my horse, you know, the chestnut gelding, was sick, and I had to tend to him. I made a whole batch of cookies, too—the chocolate ones that Hal likes. That man surely can eat cookies!"

Was a plate of cookies a reasonable exchange for a six-million-dollar contract? I wondered. And I looked at Sam, glowing and golden, and I decided that Hal probably thought so.

"By the way," I said, "thank you for changing the time. I'm afraid I overslept yesterday."

"You must have felt really bad," Sam said, looking at me with concern. "It must have been a horrible moment for you, finding him like that."

"It was pretty awful," I said. "I suppose it would have been worse if I'd actually known him, but even so . . . Did you know him?"

Her face clouded. "He was a creep," she said. "He made a pass at me once, and when I slapped him down, he got that slimy little brother of his and all his minions to make life hell for me here at Wilmot so that I'd drop out. But," she continued with a grim smile, "he chose the wrong person to try that on. I guess when I've made up my mind to do something, I usually see it through!

Besides, Linda and Dave were great, so supportive! I owe them a lot."

"Max Loring sounds as vile as his brother," I said.

"He was a sleaze," Sam said dismissively. "I can't say I'm sorry he's dead."

Indeed, there seemed to be few people who would grieve for Max Loring.

6

I was beginning to find my way about the town, and some afternoons, when I had finished classes for the day, I used to go to a little café on Main Street to eat homemade brownies and drink lemon tea. It was a delightful place, part of a kitchen shop, which sold all sorts of exciting and (to me) exotic kitchen equipment. I had already marked out a tablecloth and napkins decorated with little birds and other Pennsylvania Dutch good-luck symbols as a suitable present to take back for my friend Rosemary. A few days after the murder I was sitting there, stirring my lemon tea and idly turning the pages of the fall issue of the *Wilmot Literary Review,* when a voice at my elbow said, "Do you mind if I join you?"

I looked up and for a moment didn't recognize the man standing beside me. Then I realized that it was Lieutenant Landis. He looked different somehow, less tired, I suppose, and of course, I wasn't really expecting to see a policeman in Katy's Kitchen.

"Of course," I said. "How nice to see you. Though I'm a little surprised to find you in these feminine surroundings!"

He smiled and sat down opposite me. "I used to come here with my wife in the old days," he said, "and now—well, it's one place where no one ever thinks to look for me."

The waitress came up, and he ordered coffee and a blueberry muffin.

"Oh, dear, muffins," I said. "My one and only disappointment in America."

"I'm sorry to hear that," he said. "Don't you like them?"

"They're, well, too *cakey* if you know what I mean, like our fairy cakes, not a bit what I'd expected. Oh, and there is one other thing: cinnamon in coffee—disgusting!"

He raised his eyebrows. "And those are the only things about America that have disappointed you?" he asked.

"Well, I'm not sure about lima beans, but no, otherwise, I love everything."

"Everything? Well, we have to get you onto the Allenbrook tourist board right away. You might even run for mayor!"

We both laughed.

"You say you used to come here with your wife," I said. "Doesn't she like it here anymore?"

"She doesn't like it here," he replied, "or Allenbrook either for that matter. We're divorced. She lives in Santa Barbara now, with our daughter."

"I'm sorry." I crumbled the last of my brownie.

"I guess the job had something to do with it, too," he said. "Difficult hours, always on call, never being able to make plans—you know, all the routine things that cops say when their marriages break up, when maybe it's just incompatibility and they're ashamed to admit it."

He smiled. "How about you? Is there a Mr. Malory?"

"He died," I said, "a few years ago. I still miss him. I'm lucky, though. My son, Michael, lives at home; he works as a lawyer in the small town where I live. I suppose he'll marry and move out one day, but for the present I have company, and it's nice to have someone to look after."

He had finished his muffin and his coffee but seemed content to linger. I was curious about this policeman who seemed so very different from the hard-boiled cops in the thrillers and television serials which had, up to now, been my only source of information, so I asked, "Is Allenbrook your hometown?"

"I was born and raised in Bucks County," he said. "It's not far from here. I guess you'd call me a farm boy, though it wasn't much of a farm, just a few acres and a couple of cows. My father wasn't that interested in the farm; he was the local preacher, you see, and that kind of took all his energy. My mother and sister did what they could, and so did I, when I was old enough, but we never did more than scratch a living."

"My father was a clergyman," I said.

"An English country clergyman, like in Anthony Trollope?" he asked.

"Well, yes, I suppose so," I said, disconcerted by this plunge into English literature. "The Church of England hadn't changed all that much from its Victorian image when he died soon after the war. It's all different now, of course."

"Kind of different from my pa, too." Lieutenant Landis laughed. "He was a Lutheran, of a pretty strict sect. Life was dull for us. That's when I took to reading. The Bible on Sunday, of course, there's a lot of reading in the Bible. The only other book he allowed in the house was a complete Shakespeare. I guess he'd never actually read it himself, because there's sure a lot of things in Shakespeare my pa wouldn't have approved of! But he knew a few lines here and there and used to quote them in his preaching: 'Who steals my purse steals trash,' 'Neither a borrower, nor a lender be'—you know the kind of thing. I guess he thought the whole book was like that!"

"So *that's* what started you on Shakespeare?" I said. "Did you go to school in Allenbrook?"

"No, the public school in Lebanon. But I learned to read and write there; after that I guess it's up to you." He shrugged his shoulders. "Sure, I'd have liked to go to college and all that, but I needed to get a job, so that was that. Being a cop seemed the best way out, though I guess it was just another dead end after all. My wife used to say I had no ambition, and she was right. Allenbrook suits me. I can do without the stress and the hassle of a big city. I like to work in a small police department where I can do things my way."

"I like living in a small town, too," I said. "I like to know everyone, people I've grown up with, who know me as well. Perhaps Shakespeare came to feel like that; after all, he went back to Stratford in the end." I smiled. "I hope you manage to make your trip."

"I guess reading so much English literature," he said thoughtfully, "I'm kind of hung up on the country and the people. We don't get many British—sorry—English people in Allenbrook. Well, I guess there are some at Wilmot, but I don't usually get to meet them. That's why it's been really nice talking to you."

He smiled again, transforming his rather severe features.

"It's been nice talking to you, too," I said.

It was true, I did find these glimpses of American life fascinating, and I was curious to learn more about the lieutenant himself.

We were both silent for a moment, not really knowing what to say next, perhaps feeling that we had covered more ground than ordinary chance-met acquaintances. Then the lieutenant said hesitantly, "It would be nice to talk some more—that is, if you'd like that?"

"Yes," I said, "that would be very nice."

He leaned forward and placed his hands one on top of the other on the table. They were strong, capable-looking hands with well-kept nails. "I reckon you could help me, too—if you would."

I was startled and looked at him inquiringly.

"It's about this case, this thing at the institute. I won't say I'm out of my depth, but I don't know the people involved, there or at Wilmot. I can't make judgments about them, if you get my meaning. It would help to have someone tell me about them, someone who knows them but isn't a suspect. Someone like you from outside, who can see things with a kind of unbiased eye."

I swirled the remains of my lemon tea round in the glass and said doubtfully, "Well, I don't know most of them at all well. My friends Linda and Anna I've known for ages, but the others . . . My judgments might be quite wrong."

"It's your observations I want," he said earnestly. "I think you have a pretty good idea about what makes people tick, you've got a critical mind, and because you're a sympathetic kind of person, I guess people talk to you." He laughed. "Look at me, for instance, talking to you like this!"

"I wouldn't want . . ." I began.

"I'm not asking you to be some kind of spy or anything like that," he said hastily. "That would be a lousy thing to ask anyone, and, of course, I know Dr. Kowolski is your friend and all that. No, I just want you to tell me how you see these people, what they're like, how they react to each other, that sort of thing. It's fairly easy for you, working with them, but kind of difficult for me in a formal interview. What do you say?"

I was silent for a moment. It seemed a strange request from a policeman, and someone I had only just met. But somehow Lieutenant Landis didn't seem like a stranger. Perhaps I was flattered by his interest—not just in me, but in all things English.

"Well," I said at last, "I must confess I have a great curiosity about it all, having been in at the death, as it were. I suppose I feel somehow involved."

"That's great, Mrs. Malory." He held out his hand. "Say, can I call you Sheila, if we're going to be friends?"

"Of course," I said, and we solemnly shook hands across the table.

"My name's the same as your son's," he said, "but mine is spelled M-I-C-H-A-L, and most people call me Mike."

When Linda got back that evening, I told her about my encounter.

"Drinking tea with a literary cop in Katy's Kitchen! Whatever did you talk about?"

For some reason I couldn't quite bring myself to tell Linda what Mike Landis had asked of me. Now that I was away from his rather compelling personality it seemed just a little disloyal, so I said vaguely, "Oh, we just chatted. I think he liked talking to someone from England. He was quite cozy, really."

"Cozy?" Linda laughed. "Oh, Sheila!"

She paused in the act of opening a tin for Tiger and said, "Did he talk about the murder? How far has he got?"

"Not very far," I replied. "I think he's uncertain about how to deal with all the institute and Wilmot people. I imagine they're a bit different from his usual suspects."

Linda put the saucer of food down for Tiger, who sniffed at it and walked disdainfully away.

"I'd love to know what he makes of our Carl," she said. "Though I don't suppose," she continued regretfully, "he's a suspect. Still, you never know. He might have had some long-standing grievance against Max, way back, from childhood."

"But why would he suddenly kill him now?" I asked.

"Oh, I don't know," she replied. "Maybe something came up. I suppose I just want Carl Loring to be the murderer so we can be rid of him!"

"Can you think of anyone who *might* have had a motive?" I asked.

She shook her head. "I didn't know him well enough to say. Anna might know; she's had more to do with him than I have. But I guess a guy like that must have made a lot of enemies for a lot of reasons."

I thought of Sam. "I'm sure you're right," I replied. "I gather from Sam that *she* had a sort of run-in with him and that it was all very unpleasant."

Linda snorted. "That man—and his little toad of a brother!" she said. "Yes, they tried to make her life a misery here in the department, just because she resisted Max's advances! He certainly knew how to hold a grudge, that man."

"If he could do that to Sam," I said, "goodness knows what he's tried to do to other people who may have crossed him in some way."

"Yes," she replied, "I guess there were quite a few people at the institute who hated his guts."

I remembered Theo Portman's remark about Max Loring's having screwed things up as usual and said, "I imagine the field of suspects there is pretty wide. Perhaps Anna will be able to suggest a few."

"Well, you can ask her tomorrow," Linda said. "She's coming down for a few days. Some research she needs to do at the institute."

The next morning, just as I was leaving for the

college, the telephone rang, and a pleasant female voice said, "Mrs. Malory? This is Mr. Walter Cleveland's secretary. Mr. Cleveland apologizes for giving you such short notice, but he wonders if you would care to have lunch with him today?"

"Oh, goodness," I stammered. "Well, yes, I think I'm free. I'd love to—"

"Will you be at Wilmot College?" the voice inquired.

"Yes," I said, "yes, I will."

"That's fine, then. We'll send a car for you at twelve-thirty if that will be convenient?"

"Thank you," I replied, "that will be lovely."

I put the receiver down and rushed off to change into something more worthy. I surveyed my wardrobe in despair, wondering what I possessed that might be suitable for lunching with the head of a multinational corporation. Finally I decided on my suit, hoping that the fact that it was made of good Scottish tweed would compensate for its relative lack of chic. It would be too hot, of course, but fortunately I did have quite an elegant blouse, so I could take the jacket off, and anyway, the air-conditioning might still be on. . . . I put in a little energetic work on my hair with the curling tongs, added a bit more eye shadow than I would normally wear in class, dabbed on some scent, and dashed off to Wilmot.

Just before half past twelve an enormous black limousine drew up outside Brook Hall, and I was driven the two or three miles along the Allen River road to the Orlando headquarters. As Walter Cleveland had promised, it was a fine example of High Victorian Gothic with many turrets, crenellations and soaring stone arches, as if some over-ambitious pupil of Sir Gilbert Scott had been given unlimited funds and allowed to run riot. Inside, the reception area was housed in a vast baronial hall with a great marble staircase, and at first-floor level, there was a splendid gallery, decorated with ornate carving, from which banners (some with heraldic devices, some with the Orlando logo) hung down, like battle honors in a cathedral. Indeed, the general atmosphere was more ecclesiastical than commercial, and I wondered if some moral might be drawn about the twentieth century's worship of Mammon.

The chauffeur passed me on to a messenger who led me to a cleverly concealed lift (behind what at first sight might have been taken for a finely carved reredos) which conveyed us to a higher floor. Here we went along a corridor lined with dark linenfold paneling, and I was ushered into a room which, although decorated and furnished in splendidly nineteenth-century style, also contained a very modern desk with a computer terminal, a fax machine, and a formidable battery of telephones.

An elegant young woman got up from behind the desk to greet me. "Mrs. Malory," she said, "my name is Donna Michelson. I'm Mr. Cleveland's secretary. We spoke together this morning."

She opened a door at the far end of the room and announced, "It's Mrs. Malory, Mr. Cleveland."

I followed her into a really remarkable room.

The walls were covered with olive green watered silk, and the curtains at the long, arched windows were of the same color but of heavy velvet. The furniture was massive and intricately carved, and dominating the room was a great stone fireplace with bas-reliefs of heraldic beasts. To one side of the fireplace, set upon an easel, was a superb picture. It was painted in muted tones of brown and ocher and a dull green that was almost black. A woman sat in the foreground, one hand resting on a broken pillar, one hand laid upon her breast. Facing her was an angel, kneeling, wings folded back and with a right hand raised in salutation. Behind the figures were dark pointed trees, strangely shaped rocks, and a labyrinthine stream which curved across the background and seemed to melt into the pale ocher sky. The woman's face was as enigmatic as that of the angel confronting her, and yet there was also a powerful melancholy, echoed in the soft colors, and a mystery that caught the imagination. It was a picture one would never forget, obviously the work of a great master.

I must have stood there, gazing at it for several minutes, before I recollected myself and saw that Walter Cleveland had risen from a desk by the window and had come forward to greet me.

"I'm so sorry," I said in some confusion, shaking the hand he had extended, "I was just so—"

"I'm delighted," he said, smiling, "that you were so taken with our wonderful picture."

I turned back to look at it again. "Can it be?" I asked.

"Leonardo da Vinci, yes."

"I've never seen it reproduced anywhere," I said. "It is so beautiful, so extraordinary—I couldn't have forgotten it."

"It's quite a story," Walter Cleveland said. "It was in a private collection in Italy until quite recently. It's an early work, of course, painted when he was still in Verocchio's studio. The Uffizi has an early Annunciation—I am sure you know it— but that is in another style, more straightforward, you might say. This is the true Leonardo, or so I like to think."

"It's magnificent," I said. "You told me that you had some fine pictures here, but I hadn't expected anything like this."

Walter Cleveland smiled. "I must confess," he said, "to a little glow of pride every time I look at it, since it was I who found it for the company—"

He broke off as his secretary came into the room.

"I'm very sorry to disturb you, Mr. Cleveland," she said, "but those South American figures you wanted are just starting to come through, and you said you needed to see them as soon as possible."

"Oh, thank you, Donna. They're on your terminal, are they? Right, well, I'll just take a quick glance at them if Mrs. Malory will excuse me for one moment?"

"Of course," I replied.

"Fine. Donna will fix you a drink."

He went out of the room, and his secretary moved over to a magnificent Chinese lacquered cabinet, opened the front, and revealed an array of bottles and glasses.

"What can I get for you, Mrs. Malory?" she inquired.

"Oh, sherry would be nice. Dry, please."

She handed me a glass of Tío Pepe and asked me if I was enjoying my stay at Allenbrook, what I thought of America, did I know Northampton in England because her family had come from there way back.

As we talked, my eyes kept straying back to the Leonardo, and following my gaze, she said, "I see you're admiring our wonderful picture."

"It really is magnificent," I said. "And I gather it was Mr. Cleveland who more or less discovered it."

"He certainly did," she replied. "Someplace in Italy, near Florence. Last year."

"It was a remarkable achievement to have acquired such a masterpiece," I said, standing back to get a better view. "I imagine that there must have been quite a lot of comments about it, especially at the institute."

"Yes." She hesitated for a moment and then said, "Those so-called experts, some of them are really jealous when someone from outside—like Mr. Cleveland—makes a find like that."

"Mr. Cleveland is a very remarkable man," I said.

She gave me a warm smile. "Truly remarkable, Mrs. Malory," she said. "Of course, he is a brilliant businessman, everyone says so, but he's also a very cultivated person with fine judgment."

"But there were people at the institute who questioned that judgment?" I asked.

She hesitated and then burst out, "There was that man from the institute who practically said that the picture was a fake."

"Really!"

"Well, I didn't hear all of it. I was in my room, but the door wasn't shut all the way, and he was shouting." She looked at me quickly. "I wasn't *listening*, you know, but this man, this Max Loring, he was shouting pretty loud."

"How did Mr. Cleveland react to that?" I asked.

She shook her head. "I can't really say. He spoke quietly, you know, the way he does, so I couldn't hear. But when this guy Loring had gone, I saw his face. He had that kind of set look, the way he does when things aren't going his way in a deal and he was really upset. You can tell when

Mr. Cleveland's upset: He twists that ring of his around and around on his finger."

Her face was flushed, and she spoke vehemently. It was obvious that Donna Michelson's feelings for Walter Cleveland were stronger than those of a secretary for her employer.

"I can understand that he might well have been upset," I said sympathetically, "about a thing like that. I wonder what gave Max Loring the idea that the picture wasn't genuine."

"There was something about provenance and some old Italian family—I didn't understand—"

The telephone on the desk by the window rang suddenly, and she broke off to answer it.

"Yes, Mr. Cleveland, I'll bring her along right now."

Donna Michelson, the perfect secretary once more, turned to me and said, "Mr. Cleveland said to bring you straight to the dining room. He'll see you there."

We went up in a lift and emerged into a large circular room where Walter Cleveland was waiting.

"I do apologize for leaving you like that. I hope Donna gave you that drink?"

"Yes, indeed," I replied. Looking round me with astonishment, I continued, "What a sumptuous room!"

It was indeed amazing, paneled in dark wood, the walls hung with some very fine Dutch still-life paintings. The windows, which, since the room was circular, went all round, were high and pointed, the furniture was massively Victorian and there were great candelabra and wall sconces in gilded wood, and the floor was covered with a red and blue Turkey carpet which added to the feeling of richness and splendor.

"Come and look out of the window," Walter Cleveland said. "This room is in one of the towers, so the view is quite something."

I joined him at one of the windows and exclaimed with pleasure. Down below, the Allen River wound among the trees, and all along the valley were the great nineteenth-century mansions, each in its own wooded parkland, and far away there was a range of mountains, blue in the distance.

"You can see right over to the Delaware Water Gap," he said. "See, over there."

"What a marvelous view," I said, "and, look how the river winds—just like the river in your Leonardo!"

Over lunch I was struck again by Walter Cleveland's personality. His manner was quiet and his conversation urbane, but one was always aware of the strength and controlled power that lay underneath.

Curious about Donna Michelson's revelation, I brought the conversation around to the institute. "It was so kind of Theo to show me round," I said. "They have some really superb things, but nothing to touch your Leonardo. I expect they were very thrilled about it."

"Indeed. A little more wine? No?" He poured some wine into his own glass and continued, "Theo has asked me to allow them to put it on display there so that the public can see it. We are arranging things with the insurance company, so it will probably be some time in the spring. We thought it might form the centerpiece of a small loan exhibition of the company's finest pictures. As you can see"—he waved his hands at the paintings on the walls—"we have a fair representation of the Dutch school, and there are a couple of Cézannes and a Monet as well as an unusual Veronese."

"How splendid," I said, "and how nice that you have your pictures on display and not hidden away in some bank vault, just as assets."

"That has always seemed to me a criminal thing to do," he replied. "Pictures only have meaning if they are looked at; otherwise they are just so much paint and canvas. I shall be delighted for them to be on display to a wider public at the institute."

"It's a delightful place," I said. "Of course, they must be going through a terrible time just now, after the murder."

An expression of concern crossed his face. "Of

course," he said, "you were there when that very disturbing discovery was made. I'm so sorry."

"It was rather awful," I said. "Though I suppose it would have been worse if I'd known Max Loring. What was he like?"

There was a moment's silence, and I saw that he was twisting the heavy gold signet ring he wore on the little finger of his right hand.

"He was not a likable man," he said at last. "Arrogant, with a—what can I call it?—a very supercilious manner."

"He was their leading expert on Italian paintings, wasn't he?" I said. "What did he think of the Leonardo? He must have been very excited about such a fantastic discovery."

"He was indeed." He twisted the ring again. "In fact, he was going to write an article about it for one of the leading international art journals and, in due course, a more detailed study in book form."

He could not have known that I knew he was lying, but nevertheless, he found a way to turn the conversation, and for the rest of the lunch we discussed the various pleasures of England and Scotland ("When I go to Edinburgh for the festival, I usually try to get up to Sutherland for a few days' fishing. Do you know Helmsdale? A beautiful place") and what I should see in New York ("There is a very interesting new production of

Aïda at the Met, if you can find the time to see it").

After we had finished lunch, he took me down to the reception area himself, and as we shook hands, I said, "Thank you so much for a delightful time. It really is a wonderful building, and I'm so thrilled to have seen the Leonardo. I shall always remember it!"

He smiled and said, "I am glad you feel that the New World has something to offer."

As the car took me back to Wilmot, I found myself wondering just what had passed between Walter Cleveland and Max Loring in that stormy interview. If Loring had been right and the Leonardo *wasn't* genuine, then Walter Cleveland had a lot to lose. Not just the however many million dollars his company had paid for it, but to a man of his character, to have it made known that he had been mistaken, had been taken in, had been fooled would have been intolerable. It would have affected his standing in the company, too, since his judgment on other things must then inevitably be in question. Naturally he had taken advice from experts on the painting, but in the final analysis, the purchase had been his, and therefore, the responsibility was his as well.

To have this judgment, this responsibility questioned in a blaze of publicity (Max Loring, like his brother, would obviously relish such a situation) would be a fearsome blow. Enough of a blow to drive him to murder? Quite possibly . . .

The car drew up outside Brook Hall, and I tried to rid my mind of these speculations and concentrate on the position of the woman in the Victorian family, with especial reference to the works of Mrs. Gaskell.

7

When I got back that evening, Linda said, "The department was absolutely overcome to hear about your lunch with Walter Cleveland."

"It was marvelous," I said. "Very grand—they'll never believe it back in Taviscombe. And that Leonardo painting! It's fabulous!"

"Yes," she replied. "Anna's been dying to get a real look at it, but so far only Max Loring's had the chance."

"What did he think about it?" I asked casually.

"Oh, you know the Lorings. He was going to write an article about it, so he wasn't giving anything away beforehand!"

So Max Loring was going to explode his bombshell, his exposure of the picture (and he must have felt that his evidence was pretty strong to go into print) to the whole art world in an article. Walter Cleveland would have found that intolerable.

The telephone rang, and Linda answered it. "It's for you," she said, "your policeman."

Her eyebrows were raised quizzically as I took the telephone.

"Hello, Sheila." Mike Landis's voice was warm and friendly. "I wonder if you'd like to go over to Lancaster tomorrow morning and have a look at the market there. A lot of local color, I think you might enjoy it. And I know a good place for lunch—I promise, no muffins!"

"Well . . ." I hesitated and then said firmly, "Yes, I'd love to. That would be very nice."

"Okay. I'll pick you up about nine-thirty. I have the address."

He hung up, and I stood for a moment with the receiver in my hand, wondering just what I was getting myself into.

I went into the kitchen, where Linda was making a sauce for the linguine. "What did he want?" she asked curiously.

"He's invited me to go to Lancaster tomorrow to see the market and have lunch."

"Well, well! And are you going?"

"Yes," I said. "Yes, I am. I think it might be quite fun."

When Anna arrived and we were having supper, Linda said, "Sheila's going to Lancaster tomorrow with her new boyfriend."

"Hey!" Anna exclaimed. "What's been going on while I've been away? Who is this guy?"

"He's a cop—the lieutenant in charge of the Loring murder," Linda said.

"What!" Anna turned to me. "Is that so?"

"Don't take any notice of Linda," I said. "She's exaggerating. He's a bit of an Anglophile—he's got this thing about Shakespeare—and he's just being friendly."

When Mike arrived to collect me the next morning, I noticed that both Linda and Anna were hanging about, waiting to catch a glimpse of Mike Landis in this new role.

"You're both behaving like a couple of silly children!" I said severely as I went to answer the door. "You should be ashamed of yourselves. You'll embarrass the poor man!"

I wondered if I might feel embarrassed with him myself, but in jeans, a dark blue sweater, and a denim jacket he looked so like any member of the department that I felt perfectly relaxed and found it quite easy to call him Mike.

We drove through dairy country, occasionally passing Amish families in their horse-drawn buggies—the men dressed in black with beards and shovel-shaped hats like Victorian curates, the women also in black, with white caps.

"A lot of them have stalls in the market," Mike said, "for produce they've grown or made."

The market was wonderful: glorious displays of richly colored fruit and vegetables, delicious-looking cheeses, bread and cakes, and huge containers of apple juice. There were other stalls, too, piled high with lovely lacework and a lot of cushions, quilts, and covers all decorated with little red hearts. These stalls were presided over by fresh-faced young Amish girls, who wore their long black dresses with fine white collars and white lawn caps so naturally that they didn't seem to be wearing fancy dress at all, as I had thought they might. I spent quite a lot of money.

When we had wandered round the market and Mike had waited patiently while I had a good browse in a splendid bookshop, he led the way to a very folksy restaurant, all red-and-white gingham tablecloths and tablemats decorated with Amish hearts.

"Goodness," I said, as we took our places in one of the high-backed booths, "first Katy's Kitchen, now this. Do you like country and western music, too?"

He gave a sudden grin, quite different from his usual slow smile. "Yes, well, I guess I do find this kind of place a nice change from the kind of bars where I have to spend too much of my time. Actually, the food here is really good."

He guided me through the menu ("No, that'll have cinnamon in it, you wouldn't like it . . . and you have to have shoofly pie—it's a little sweet and sticky, but you must try it just once! And you must drink our local cider—it's okay, it's really like apple juice"), and then he said, "Well, isn't this something!"

I smiled and took a sip of my cider. "You're

right," I said, "it is like apple juice. One day you must come to the West Country and try *our* cider. Now that really is strong, especially the kind they still brew in some of the local farmhouses; a couple of glasses would put you away!"

"Perhaps I will come, one day," he said.

After we had finished our meal (the shoofly pie *was* very sticky), I said, "How is the case going? Have you made much progress?"

He pushed his coffee cup to one side and said, "Well, now. There was something I wanted to show you."

He reached into the inside pocket of his jacket and produced a plastic wallet from which he took out a letter and handed it to me. "We found this in Max Loring's desk. I hoped you might be able to identify the person it was written to."

The letter was printed on computer paper and read:

Thursday

My Dear Sam,

So you're getting married. I wonder if your Hal knows about us? After all, there was a lot of gossip around Wilmot, wasn't there? And there's usually no smoke without fire. I'm sure Hal would think so (didn't someone tell me that he is a very jealous kind of person?). Will he believe you if you deny it, as I'm sure you

*will? No doubt your readings in great litera-
ture will provide you with many instances of
jealousy that had unfortunate results (Othello,
for instance). Not that Hal would actually
strangle you, of course. I am sure he is far too
civilized, but perhaps that substantial settlement might not materialize.*

*I do feel we should meet for a little chat
sometime soon to see if a solution might be
found that is agreeable to us both—not necessarily financial.*

I look forward to hearing from you. Soon.

Yours,

Max.

"Oh, no!" I exclaimed when I had read the
letter. "Poor Sam—how utterly *unspeakable*!"

Mike looked at me sharply. "You know who it's
addressed to?"

I realized that by my exclamation I had given
away any hope of pretending I didn't know who
the recipient of the letter might be. "Yes," I said.
"It's one of my graduate students, Samantha
Broderick."

"Ah . . ." He beckoned the waitress over. "More
coffee?"

There was a silence while more coffee was
poured, and then I said, "Do you think he actually
sent that letter?"

"He might have. This could be a copy he took. I didn't find any reply, but I guess she might have telephoned."

"There's no proper date?" I asked.

"No," he replied. "That struck me as odd, but then I looked at some of his other correspondence, and though he dated his business letters, he only put the day of the week on his private correspondence—some sort of affectation, I guess."

"If he was anything like his brother," I said, "he was probably a mass of affectations."

"So what is this settlement, then?" he persisted.

"Oh," I said as casually as I could, "I believe it's some sort of—what do they call it over here?—*prenuptial* settlement. We don't have that sort of thing—well, only in very upper-class families where there's a lot of property and so forth."

"Is this Hal a rich man, would you say?"

"I don't really know," I said. "I believe he has some sort of farm," I added, trying to make it sound like a very tiny smallholding. "Anyway," I continued, "there never was an affair. Loring certainly pursued Sam, pretty vigorously, I believe, but she turned him down flat. I daresay he found it hard to forgive her for that—very sure of themselves, both the Lorings! There *was* quite a bit of gossip around the department, you know how these places are, but that was all."

"And is this Hal a jealous kind of guy?" Mike

asked. "I mean, do you think he'd take Loring's word that they'd had an affair, even if she denied it?"

"I don't know," I replied. "I've never met him. It seems a flimsy enough threat to me."

"With a person who's really jealous it doesn't take much," he said.

" 'Trifles light as air/Are to the jealous confirmations strong/As proofs of holy writ,' you mean," I said.

"Othello." He took the quotation. "Perhaps that's why Loring mentioned that in his note: to emphasize the point."

There was a pause while Mike stirred his coffee and I fiddled with a little dish of very pale butter that the waitress hadn't removed.

"Was this Sam Broderick at the concert?" Mike asked.

"No," I replied, "I'm quite sure she wasn't. In fact," I went on, fluent now with relief, "it was a fairly exclusive occasion—only for college faculty and members of the institute, of course, and important visitors like Walter Cleveland."

"She couldn't have slipped in somehow?" he suggested.

"The security guards were very careful to check our invitation cards," I said. "I suppose the security there has to be pretty strict—I mean, all those valuable things."

"I guess so."

He sounded disappointed, and I felt he was reluctant to let go of a possible suspect.

"Have your forensic people worked out the time of the murder?" I asked.

"Well"—he gave a little grimace—"it's not that straightforward. What with the special air-conditioning and the fact that the body was in that airtight chest, it's not easy to be accurate. It seems most likely that he was killed between three and seven o'clock, though it *could* have been earlier."

"Just before the concert, then," I said. "So you have to look for your suspect among the guests."

I paused and then said, "I think I *may* have a suspect for you."

I felt a little mean, telling Mike about Walter Cleveland and the possibly fake Leonardo, but I decided it might divert his attention from Sam. Anyway, I was sure Walter Cleveland was more than capable of looking after himself in any investigation.

"Do you think this secretary would testify to what she heard?" he asked.

"She might not," I said. "I sort of got the impression that she's very devoted to him. That's why she couldn't resist telling me how clever he was and how it was only jealousy and envy that made the so-called expert say that he was wrong."

"Still," he said thoughtfully, "if one expert could spot a thing like that, I guess we could get others to have a look at the picture."

"So you'll follow it up?" I asked.

"Sure, I follow up everything. Thanks, Sheila." He gave me a friendly smile. "Though," he continued ruefully, "I'd rather have a less powerful and influential suspect. I'll have to step really carefully on this one!"

"Is there anything else you're following up?" I asked. "I mean, if you're allowed to tell me."

"Well, there is one of the oldest motives in the world," he said.

"Money?"

"Money," he agreed. "It seems that this Max Loring was a rich man. Not in money as such, but he had a lot of objects, pictures, sculpture, and stuff like that, and our experts think they're worth a lot of dollars."

"I expect," I suggested, "he used his position at the institute to ferret out all sorts of art treasures that people didn't know the value of and then bought them cheaply."

"From what I hear," Mike said, "he sounds like that kind of guy."

"So," I inquired, "who gets the money? His brother, Carl?"

"Carl." Mike nodded. "Who, it seems, went to see his brother at the institute on the day of the murder and was heard to have a very noisy fight with him."

"No! Goodness! What was it about?" I asked.

Mike shrugged. "That's the trouble. We can't

find out. All I can get is the raised angry voices; nobody got the actual words." He gave me a sideways smile and said, "So there we are, 'gravelled for lack of matter.' "

"Oh, wait a minute." I searched through my memory. "*Much Ado About Nothing*? No, hang on, I'm sure it's one of the comedies. *Twelfth Night*?"

"No, it's *As You Like It*. Rosalind." He smiled again. "No, several people heard them shouting in Loring's office, and one of the security guards remembers seeing Carl Loring leaving the institute looking really upset."

"Did they have any other family?" I asked.

"No, their parents are both dead. Carl is his brother's heir; he gets everything."

"Perhaps they quarreled about money," I suggested. "From what I've seen Carl has pretty expensive tastes, and if Max was that well off, then maybe . . ."

"Somehow Max doesn't strike me as an easy touch," Mike said. "Not even for a brother."

"So I wonder what it was. You can never tell with families, what upsets people and so on."

"Yes," he said, "you can never tell."

We fell silent, and after a moment I asked, "Do you see your daughter at all?"

"Weekends, sometimes," he replied. "She's in college now, Berkeley. Sometimes in the school breaks we meet in New York. We stay with my sister; she's got an apartment on Central Park

West. She's divorced, too. We don't seem to be able to make it in my family, do we?"

"What's your daughter's name?" I asked.

"Laura."

He took out his wallet and produced a photograph of a girl wearing tennis clothes. She had long blond hair caught back in a band, and she had Mike's smile.

"She's very pretty," I said. "Is she very good at tennis?"

"They thought she had promise when she was a kid," he said, "and her mother wanted her to go for it—professionally, I mean. But I didn't want her to. Well, you know how it is. It takes over their lives; they never have time to be kids, to enjoy growing up naturally; the pressures are tremendous. Sure, they make a lot of money, but it's all so *narrow*. What kind of people do they turn into? That's one of the things that split us up, I guess. Emma, that's my wife, was very ambitious, for herself and for Laura; she was all for moving to California, tennis schools, you know how it goes. I couldn't do that, and I didn't want it for my daughter. So she left and took Laura with her."

"So what happened about the tennis?" I asked.

"Oh, Laura wasn't really good enough. She won a couple of small competitions, but that was it. She's majoring in economics and math—going to be an accountant."

"Oh, well"—I laughed—"so she'll be making a lot of money anyway, without the tennis!"

On the way back to Allenbrook Mike said, "I'm due to see Carl Loring on Monday. I saw him, just to tell him that his brother had been murdered and to get a brief statement, but I need to have a real talk now."

"And you'll see Walter Cleveland, too?"

"Sure. And Samantha Broderick."

"Well," I said firmly, "I should think that Carl Loring's your best bet. After all, most crimes are domestic, don't they say? And money *is* the root of all evil!"

He gave me a sideways glance and said, "Now why do I get the impression that you'd like Carl Loring to be the murderer?"

"Well, he is the most unlikable of your three suspects and really a pretty repellent person."

"I'm afraid life isn't like that," he replied. "I've known some very pleasant murderers."

" 'There's no art/To find the mind's construction in the face,' " I suggested.

"*Macbeth,*" he responded absently. "Still, we haven't explored all the possibilities yet. I got the impression from the curator, Theo Portman, that Max Loring was generally unpopular there. Who knows what motives we may yet turn up?"

8

"So, come on, tell us what the hot news is!" Linda said when I got back. "Is an arrest imminent? Or," she added with a sideways glance, "were you so taken up with each other that you never mentioned the murder?"

"Don't be ridiculous," I replied austerely.

"So, stop stalling. Tell!" she insisted.

I hesitated for a moment; then I said, "Mike Landis has found a letter from Loring to Sam, threatening to tell Hal that they were having an affair."

"He did what!" Linda shrieked. "But how could he? She hated him!"

"General malice," I replied, "revenge, or maybe a bit of discreet blackmail. He knew about the settlement."

"The slimeball!" Anna said with venom.

"Fortunately," I said, "it seems that Sam couldn't have been in the institute—I don't think she was invited to the concert, was she?—when

Loring was murdered, so even though she had a motive, there doesn't seem to have been an opportunity, thank goodness."

"So who else is in the frame?" Anna asked.

"You'll like this," I said. "Carl Loring."

"Well, of course, we'd all *love* to think he did it," Linda said, "but is there any reason for the police to suspect him?"

"He's his brother's sole heir," I said, "and Max Loring had some pretty valuable things, I believe. *Also,* they were heard having a tremendous row on the day of the murder."

"Hey," Linda said, "that's better! What was this fight about?"

"That's the trouble," I replied. "No one seems to know. They just heard the shouting but couldn't make out the words."

"I wonder . . ." Linda began. "I might just make a stab at what it could have been. Do you want some herbal tea?"

"No, thanks," I said, "I'm still full of shoofly pie. Go *on*!"

"Well," she said, "Carl Loring had this idea about getting some prestigious international theater company over here to do a season at Wilmot."

"Good heavens!" I exclaimed. "Talk about delusions of grandeur! I mean, Wilmot's a marvelous place, but—well!"

"Empire building again," Linda said. "It would have cost a fortune in guarantees and stuff, and then the theater here is quite good for a small college but nowhere near well equipped enough for a major company, so it would have needed a new lighting system and heaven knows what all." She fished a teabag out of her mug and put it in the bin.

"So?" I prompted her.

"So," she said, "he needed to raise a lot of money. It just so happened I was sitting in the next booth to him and Rick Johnson in the Blue Moon Diner the other morning, and I heard them discussing it. You can imagine how Loring enjoyed showing off to a little creep like Rick. He was going on about all these glamorous plans and how maybe they could expand the cinema side of things—a larger, better-equipped theater would help Rick, too—and the little toad was just eating it up. Then he asked the big, hard question. Where was the money coming from?"

"Good question," Anna said.

"Oh, Loring said, that was easy. They'd raise it from local business sources. All it needed was one big initial donation, and the rest would come flooding in."

"Could be," Anna agreed.

"And, Loring said, he could get that first donation from his brother."

Anna snorted. "Fat chance!" she said.

"That's what I thought," Linda replied, "but then he went on to say that brother Max had just sold the family home in Washington (apparently he'd taken it over when their mother died and he'd been working at Georgetown), and Loring figured that half of that money was due to him."

"And," I said excitedly, "presumably Max refused to hand over the money, and they had a terrific bust-up!"

"You see! It all fits in," Linda said excitedly. "And Loring was so obsessed with this plan of his he'd do anything to make it succeed."

"Even murder?" I asked.

"Well, you've seen the guy in action; you know what he's like. Has to have his own way, by any means, and anything for the greater glorification of Loring."

"But his own brother!" I said.

"They weren't that close, and anyway, he'd have thought it was his *right*—half share of a family inheritance. No, what you have to do now, Sheila, is to call that nice cop of yours and tell him you know what the fight was about."

"Oh, well"—I hesitated—"he's off duty; he won't be at the police station."

"You're not going to tell me that he hasn't given you his home number," Linda said.

"Yes, well . . ."

"Well, then!" Linda said. "Get moving! You can use the phone in my study; you'll be quite private there!"

She and Anna exchanged smiles, and I said with

dignity, "I certainly couldn't have a serious conversation about murder suspects with you two giggling away like a couple of schoolgirls!"

Mike sounded surprised to hear from me but, I thought, pleased.

"First," I said, "I'd like to thank you for a lovely day."

"It was my pleasure. To tell the truth, I haven't enjoyed myself so much for years. You're very good company, Mrs. Malory, do you know that?"

"It was fun," I said, and went on quickly. "Actually, the main reason I'm telephoning is that I think I may have found out why Max and Carl Loring were quarreling."

I told him what Linda had said and what she had overheard.

"Well, now," he replied, "that's pretty interesting. When I'm on a case I always like to hear about people falling out over money; it's a real, solid motive. Money is good news."

" 'Money is like muck, not good except it be spread,' " I said.

"Hey, you've got me there," he said. "I can't think what *that's* from."

"I cheated," I said, laughing. "It's not Shakespeare. It's Bacon, though there are some who'll tell you that's the same thing."

"I just don't believe those guys," Mike said. "Shakespeare is Shakespeare, and you'll never convince me otherwise."

"You'll feel that even more strongly when you've been to Stratford," I said.

"I'm even more determined to go now," he said. "Now that *you* can show me around."

"So when are you seeing Carl Loring?" I asked.

"Monday afternoon. I wanted to make a few inquiries about his financial situation, and I'll have to check with his bank, especially now. I'll let you know how it goes. Maybe you'll be in Katy's Kitchen late Monday afternoon?"

"Well, yes, I might be ... I think I can hear Linda calling. I have to go now."

Although I was deeply curious about the outcome of the interview with Carl Loring, and I knew that Linda and Anna would expect me to find out all I could, I wasn't sure that seeing Mike again was a good idea. Of course, I wasn't affected by Linda and Anna's teasing, I told myself; that was all nonsense, really. But I had felt quite strongly, when I was with Mike, that he was beginning to regard me as more than just a visitor from England who happened to share his interest in Shakespeare. He was a pleasant person, very pleasant indeed, but he was a lonely man, who might read more than was meant into a chance acquaintance. I was enjoying my time at Wilmot— I liked my students and most of the people in the department, and I loved Linda and Anna as dear friends—but it was only an interlude, and at the end of several months I would be going home to my real life. Anything else was a complication I could do without. The trouble was that now I had somehow, by my own natural curiosity, got myself into the situation where I was (in however minor a way) involved in the investigation of Max Loring's murder. Actually I didn't feel like giving up on that. I would simply have to watch my step with Mike Landis.

"So?" Linda said when I went back into the kitchen, where she and Anna were getting supper. "What did he say?"

"He's going to see Carl on Monday afternoon," I told her. "I suppose he'll go and see Sam, too. I hope she isn't wearing all her diamonds when he does. I tried to give the impression that Hal was just a simple farmer and that the settlement was no big deal. Still," I continued, "I think I've persuaded Mike Landis that she couldn't have got into the institute anyway."

But later on that evening, when Linda was teasing Anna again about her overstuffed handbag, I suddenly remembered the missing invitation card. Anna had been in the department common room, and Sam had been in and out of there, too. The invitation card could easily have fallen out of Anna's bag, and if Sam had seen it, she might have decided that it would be the perfect way to get into the institute unobtrusively and deal with Max Loring. Whether or not Sam was capable of murder I wasn't sure, but she certainly had a strong motive.

I had a lovely Sunday with Linda and Anna, driving about the Pennsylvania countryside, crisscrossed with charming little covered bridges, admiring the neat farmhouses and barns and the sleek black and white cattle. We had lunch with Sara Heisick and her husband at the millhouse they had converted, with a great carved wooden stairway and a millpond (complete with trout) actually inside the house. Afterwards I was taken out into the woods that surrounded the house and solemnly shown some poison ivy, that harmless-looking three-leaved plant that I was told could wreak such havoc.

"Charles and I had a terrible time this summer," Sara said. "We thought we'd got the yard clear of it, and fool that I was, I didn't wear gloves one time when I pulled up some weeds—and there I was covered with these hellish blisters. That was just about the time when Carl Loring was pushing that terrible policy document about an expository writing course—all that crap about territories of voice and conflict within cultural questions. Do you remember, Linda? And those *endless* committee meetings we had to sit through just because Rob Huron was too feeble to say no. I was nearly crazy with the irritation of the poison ivy *and* Loring going *on* about students' learning to recognize the rhetorical situation! If it hadn't been for Dave cutting him down to size, reminding him that his area was strictly limited to drama and that he didn't have jurisdiction over that area of teaching—not as yet, anyway."

"Yes," Linda agreed, "Dave really outmaneuvered him, but Loring's had it in for him ever since."

"I know," Sara said. "All the old tricks: putting students up to complain about his courses, attacking Dave as a former director of freshman comp and the way he ran things, putting up suggestions for programs that would undercut Dave's specializations—the lot. It's all quite vile, because Dave's been through a really bad time lately, what with losing Elaine like that and worrying about the children. Only a slimebucket like Loring would add to his troubles! And now Loring's trying to edge him out of the college policy committee. It's something we can't let happen. But it's so exhausting having to fight Loring all the time, when, God knows, there's far too much else to do! Hell, why are we wasting our time talking about that creep. What about a slice of apple pie and a cup of coffee?"

I didn't have any early classes on Monday morning, so after Linda left, I sat down to write to Michael. I'd just finished describing the old millhouse ("There was a great wooden table made out of a whole circle cut from a tree. And all the latches on the doors were hand-carved—perhaps we could try that on the pantry door") when Anna came into the kitchen in search of coffee.

"Hi. I overslept, would you believe it? Oh, there's some juice." She reached into the fridge and took out a carton. "Oh, cranberry—yuk—isn't there any orange?"

"Yesterday was nice," I said. "I do like Sara and Charles and that heavenly house!"

I got up and reached past her to find the orange juice. "There," I said, pouring out a glass for both of us. "Have you been out jogging yet?" I asked.

"No, there's no time now. I thought I'd jog gently in to the institute instead. I'll cover about the same distance."

I looked at her tracksuit and trainers. "Won't you be a bit informally dressed for the institute?" I asked.

Anna laughed. "It's not exactly the Bodleian Library, you know," she said. "And I guess tracksuits are a sort of student uniform now, even for formal wear. They've kind of taken over from jeans."

"Come to think of it," I said, "when Michael was up at Oxford, he used to turn up at the Bodleian in his motorcycle gear, leathers, boots, crash helmet, and all! I'm just writing to him now. Have you any message?"

"Give him my love. Oh, and tell him I've got another crazy American name for him. I was at a two-day conference last week at a little college in upstate New York—a place called Chicopee Falls."

"Oh, how gorgeous. He'll love that!" I exclaimed. Michael and Anna had this running joke about English and American place-names and which country could produce the most extraordinary ones.

"Tell him from me," Anna said, "that I think that's at least equal to his Toller Porcorum and Chilton Cantelo! Hell, is that the time! I must be off."

She snatched up her handbag and a couple of files and rushed out, returning in a moment with Tiger. "Look who was on the porch—out all night again last night!"

Tiger, anxious to see what if anything had materialized on his plate in his absence, wriggled impatiently in her grasp.

"Ouch!" she cried, putting him down hastily. "You monster! Look what you've done!" She exhibited a long scratch on her hand and went to rinse it off under the tap.

"Are you all right?" I asked. "Shall I see if I can find you a Band-Aid?"

"No, it's fine; it's stopped bleeding now—I must dash. Bye."

Tiger, affronted by a still-empty plate, wound himself round my legs, opening and shutting his mouth silently. Used as I was to a very vocal Siamese, I always found this ploy irresistible.

"Very well, you wicked creature," I said, going to the fridge and getting out his bowl of cooked chicken. "First things first."

It was a lovely, bright sunny day when I drove into Wilmot. I'd hired a car when I first arrived and was now reasonably confident about driving on the wrong side of the road, though I still tended to panic a bit at junctions—I couldn't get used to traffic lights way up in the air and not at eye level—and I hadn't dared to tackle a freeway yet, but all in all, I felt reasonably competent as I swung into a blessedly free parking space at Brook Hall.

My class was at twelve o'clock, and it was now about ten minutes to, a time when everything should have been quiet, with students in classes or conferences. But to my astonishment there were people everywhere, and as I got out of the car, I saw that the entrance to the department was cordoned off with white tapes and a policeman was on duty at the door. I edged my way through the crowd of excited students and found Sara talking to Ted Stern.

"What on earth's going on?" I asked.

Sara gave a slightly hysterical little laugh. "Someone's finally got to Carl Loring," she said. "He's been murdered."

9

As we stood there, all three of us stunned by the unexpectedness of the event, making the sort of disjointed remarks that such a situation seems to produce, Mike Landis appeared in the doorway with another policeman. He looked at the figures milling around outside and came over to us. Nodding briefly at Sara and Ted, he said to me, "Oh, Mrs. Malory, can you spare me a few minutes, please?" He turned to the policeman at his side. "Schwartz, clear all these people away. I'll be in the secretary's office if anyone needs me."

He turned and led the way inside, and I followed, not quite knowing how to respond to Sara's and Ted's raised eyebrows and questioning glances. "They've given me this office to use for now," Mike said. He gestured towards a hot plate with a percolator on it. "Do you want some coffee?"

"No," I said. "No, thanks. Mike, what's happened?"

He put the cup of coffee he had poured for himself down carefully on a file so that it wouldn't mark the polished surface of the desk. "Someone has put a knife in Carl Loring's ribs," he said, "and killed him." For a moment I didn't take in what Mike had said; the words seemed to have no meaning.

I sat down in the chair facing him. "Where?" I asked. "Here, in the department?"

"Yes. In the kitchen of the common room."

I shook my head as if that would make things clearer. "When was it? Did anyone see anything?"

"It's more or less only just happened. It must have been sometime between ten and ten-thirty. People were in the common room until just before ten and he was found at about ten-forty, when someone"—he consulted some notes in front of him—"someone called Dave Hunter went into the kitchen and found him."

"Dave?"

"Yes." He paused. "It seems that this guy Hunter went into the common room around ten-thirty. He sat there for a while, reading or something. Then he said he wanted a cup of coffee, so he went into the kitchen to make one and found Loring lying there. Hunter said that he was dead when he found him."

"So the murder must have been committed before ten-thirty?" I suggested.

"Unless Hunter was the murderer," he replied.

"Oh, no!" I exclaimed. "Not Dave, it couldn't be. He's, well, too *gentle* to do anything like that."

Mike smiled. "I guess you're really not a lot of help on a murder case, Sheila. You always see the good side of everyone."

"Well," I said, "I don't suppose you'll find many people who can see the good side of Carl Loring! He wasn't what you'd call popular."

"Did Dave Hunter dislike him?" Mike asked.

"Yes, he did," I replied, "but then so did practically everyone else in the department. Loring really was a thoroughly nasty piece of work."

"So a lot of people would have liked him dead?" he persisted.

"If you're looking for suspects," I said, "I should think you'll be spoiled for choice. No, seriously, he was the sort of man who actually enjoyed making enemies."

"Including his brother," Mike said.

"Oh, goodness, yes!" I said excitedly. "You were going to see him this afternoon about that quarrel. Well, I suppose this means he didn't murder his brother."

"Not necessarily," he replied. "The two murders may be completely separate. Unless you can think of anyone who wanted both of them out of the way?"

"No," I said, trying to think clearly. "Unless there's someone who'd inherit from both of them."

"I haven't checked out Carl Loring's will yet," he said, "but there aren't any other relations. There were just the two of them in that family."

We sat in silence for a moment. Then I said, "Of course, most people would have been in classes or conferences around then, so I expect pretty well everyone will have alibis."

"Yes, except for this Hunter guy, though I guess there may be others. I'll be checking that, of course."

"The department is usually pretty quiet between classes," I said, "so you may not be able to find anyone who saw the murderer go in and out of the common room. Was there any other way into the kitchen?"

"There's a door that leads out into the furnace room," he said, "but apparently that's always locked. So, no, whoever it was had to go through the common room."

"Did anyone see Loring going into the common room?" I asked.

"Haven't found anyone so far. He'd been to see the chair of the department, what's his name?"

"Rob Huron."

"Yes, Huron," he said, "just before nine o'clock. Some sort of administrative matter, Huron said—I'll have to get more details of that—and no one saw him after that."

He gave me a sudden smile. When he relaxed like this, his rather formidable manner softened, allowing a glimpse of the kind and sensitive nature that it concealed. I somehow felt that not many people had seen this side of Mike's character for some time—not, perhaps, since his wife had left—and possibly, given the circumstances of her leaving, well before that.

I found that I was instinctively smiling back.

"It helps a lot, Sheila," he said, "to talk it through like this. You know these people, and you know the—what should I call it?—the *atmosphere* of the place. I'm a great believer in getting the atmosphere right. It can tell you more about a case sometimes than all the statements can! And talking to you about it sure as hell is an improvement on hacking away at it alone."

"What about your colleagues?" I inquired.

"That's not the way I work," he said. "On a murder case you need one mind, kept clear, concentrating on that and nothing else."

"Well, of course," I said, "anything I can do to help . . ."

"That's nice," he said. "Look, why don't we have dinner tomorrow evening? There's this place in the center of town, serves really good Thai food. I think you'd like it. By then I should have gotten a lot more facts, and we can puzzle them out together."

My instinct to avoid a tête-à-tête with Mike battled briefly with my curiosity. The curiosity won.

"That would be lovely," I said.

*   *   *

Most of the members of the department, denied access to the common room and badly needing a place to congregate and discuss this extraordinary happening, drifted one by one into the cafeteria building. Even people who didn't normally eat lunch, like Linda, were there.

"I still can't believe it," she said, picking the anchovy out of her Caesar salad. "I mean, the guy was a creep, right? We all hated him, but it's really terrible to think that he's been *murdered*."

Sara and Ted Stern, who were sitting at our table, gave murmurs of assent.

"An awful lot of people have reason to be glad he's dead, though," Ted said, voicing what we were all thinking but, perhaps, couldn't quite bring ourselves to put into words. "Practically every member of the department."

"It's just as well, then," I said, "that most people will have been in class and will have an alibi. I haven't, of course"—I laughed—"but then I suppose I haven't been at Wilmot long enough to have a motive!"

"Why did the lieutenant want to speak to you just now?" Sara asked curiously.

Linda laughed. "Didn't you know? He's Sheila's new boyfriend—very smitten, he is."

"It's not like that," I protested. "It was just something"—I searched around for some plausible explanation—"something about some books I was recommending. He's a great Anglophile, and he's planning a trip next year," I improvised hastily. The last thing I wanted was for my colleagues in the department to think that I was, for any reason, in league with the police. "Actually I *was* able to find out a little bit of what he's turned up so far."

I told them about Dave Hunter finding the body.

"Do you think the lieutenant suspects Dave?" Linda asked anxiously.

"He doesn't really think anything yet," I said. "He's still pretty confused about who's who in the department. I suppose he'll be interviewing everyone soon—to see where they were and so forth."

"Yes," Sara said. "There's a list of times he wants to see everyone this afternoon, put up in the office. Oh, well, I'm okay. I was in my Chaucer class from ten to eleven o'clock. How about you, Ted?"

"Robert Lowell and confessional poetry," he replied, "a poor course but mine own. Only four students this semester, but I guess that will suffice for an alibi! What about you, Linda?"

Linda shrugged. "Well, no. I should have had a conference with Gina, but she never showed up. She's usually so conscientious, works really hard, but just lately—well, you've seen it, too, Sheila, haven't you?—there's been a lack of concentration. She hasn't been writing up her material . . ."

She pushed the uneaten remains of the salad around her plate and sat silently for a moment. "I guess I was worried about her," she went on finally. "I waited a bit, and then I went to the secretary's room to see if she'd called in sick, but there was no word there. So I just wandered around the department, looking for her. Then at about ten forty-five I came back to my office and tried to call her at home, but there was no reply. I'd just put down the phone when I heard all the racket down the hall by the common room, shouting and people running, so I went out to see what it was. So I don't have an alibi for the time of the murder. . . ." Her voice trailed away.

"Well," Sara said robustly, "no one in their right mind would think that *you* murdered anyone!"

"Nor do you have a motive," Ted said. "At least, no more than the rest of us."

"For that matter," I said frivolously, "I might have had a motive. After all, Carl Loring was in England quite often. Who knows what he was up to while he was there!"

"Say," Ted said, "that's quite an idea! No, I don't mean you, Sheila. But he did have a long spell at Toronto before he came to Wilmot. Just because he looked so young, you sort of forget that Loring has been around quite a while. He must have been in his late forties. Max was in his mid-fifties. I know, because he was in Vietnam, if you can imagine such a thing! So someone in the department might have known Loring in Canada—someone who's only come here quite recently."

"You mean Rick Johnson," Sara said thoughtfully. "But he's always sucked up to Loring."

"It might be a front," Ted replied, "to throw him off the scent."

"Well," Linda said, "I've no doubt the lieutenant will go into everyone's past history. He seems a pretty thorough sort of guy to me. What do you say, Sheila?"

"Oh, yes," I replied. "I don't think he misses much."

There was little work done that afternoon. Those members of the department who were not being interviewed by the police hung about, talking in low tones and casting sidelong glances at each other. What might be termed the anti-Loring faction clung together, slightly defiant, it seemed to me, as though they felt the suspicion of the other group. Rob Huron passed among them, with an emollient word here, a bland smile there. In spite of the disruption to the department, he seemed almost to be relishing the situation, as if he felt it somehow increased his importance.

I decided I might as well go home. Down in the parking lot I ran into Sam, who had just arrived. She was looking quite subdued for her. Her clothes were as elegant as ever (cream trousers and a loose coffee-colored cotton sweater), and the diamonds were in place, but her usual vivacity and sparkle were notably absent.

"Hi." She spoke almost listlessly.

"Hello, Sam," I said. "Is anything the matter?"

"That bastard Loring!" she said bitterly.

"Loring?"

"Yeah, Max Loring. He was trying to, well, sort of blackmail me, and now the police think I murdered him. They're going to be asking Hal all sorts of questions about things I don't want him to know. Loring threatened to tell Hal that we'd had an affair, though there was no way . . . But Hal's crazy jealous, and he might just have believed him. If the police ask him about it, well, that might be it. I know the man!"

"It's just possible the police will be too busy at the moment to follow that one up," I said.

"Why?" She looked startled. "What do you mean?"

"Haven't you heard?" I asked. "*Carl* Loring's just been murdered."

"What!" Sam turned her intense blue gaze on me. "Where? When?"

"Here in the common room, well, in the kitchen there, this morning, about ten o'clock. Hadn't you heard?"

"No. I was here around nine; I wanted to pick up some books from the library. Well, I got them, and then I went back to the farm to finish off some work before this afternoon's conference with Linda. I've just got back here."

"Was Hal at home this morning?" I asked.

"No," she said. "He's away in Philadelphia for a couple of days. Why?"

"Oh, nothing," I said. "It's just that everyone in the department is being asked about their alibis."

"Well, I'm sure as hell not sorry that both Lorings are dead, but why should I want to kill Carl?"

"No reason," I said hastily. "I just thought I'd better tell you."

"Sure," she said. "Thanks."

"I don't know if there'll *be* any conferences or classes or, indeed, if there'll be anything at all going on here this afternoon," I said. "The police have cordoned off parts of the building, and the lieutenant is going to be interviewing people for most of the time. I expect he'll want to see you, too. Come to think of it, it might be easier for you to see him here rather than at the farm with Hal around."

"You're right," she said. "I'll go and see him."

"By the way," I said as she turned to go, "have you seen Gina this morning?"

"Gina?" She stopped and looked at me inquiringly.

"Yes," I went on, "she seems to have disappeared. She had a conference with Linda at ten, but she never turned up, and she doesn't seem to be at home. Linda called her there. It's a bit awkward, really, because she should have been Linda's alibi for the time Loring was killed—that was between ten and ten-forty . . ."

Sam hesitated, and then she said quickly, "No, I haven't seen her. Like I said, I wasn't around here long. She wasn't in the library, that's for sure."

I had a strong feeling that she wasn't telling the truth, but for the life of me I couldn't imagine why she should be lying.

"Oh, well," I said vaguely, "I daresay there's a perfectly simple explanation."

Linda and I had been going to meet Anna in town for a hamburger and then go on to see a film.

"Should we still go?" I suggested tentatively to Linda as we sat in her office, drinking coffee and going over once again the extraordinary events of the day.

"Well," Linda said robustly, "it would be pretty hypocritical for me to pretend I'm in any way grief-stricken at Loring's murder! So I figure a trip to McDonald's and an evening at the movies aren't going to make me seem some sort of unfeeling wretch."

The door opened, and Dave Hunter came in. "Hi," he said, "I've come for coffee and sympathy. I've just been grilled by the good lieutenant, and I'm beginning to feel like suspect number one."

Linda spooned some coffee powder into a mug,

filled it up with water from a jug, and put it in the microwave.

"Won't be a minute," she said as she pressed various buttons (the functioning of the microwave is as mysterious and unfathomable to me as that of the nuclear reactor). "My coffee machine's not working, so we're having to improvise. So. What's with the lieutenant?"

"It was my fault, I guess," Dave said ruefully. "He was asking me about Loring, you know, as a person and a teacher, and I'm afraid I let slip just how I feel about all that crap about this new system of grading and the bad effect it would have on the department. And I sort of got carried away—you know how I do?"

The microwave gave a little ping, as if of agreement, and Linda took out the cup of coffee and gave it to Dave.

"So before I knew what I was saying, like a fool I was telling him all about the fight over freshman comp and the way Loring was trying to take over on the policy committee. . . ."

"Oh, Dave!" Linda said.

"I don't know that's such a bad thing," I suggested. "*I* think he'll take it as a proof of total innocence. After all, if you *were* the murderer, you'd hardly go right in and give yourself a motive the very first time he interviewed you, now would you?"

"Unless he was very cunning and it was a double bluff," Linda said, smiling affectionately at him.

He smiled back, his rather austere face lighting up as it always did when he looked at Linda. As they sat there chatting, I found myself regarding them like a fond matchmaking mama. They would be so well suited, both rather reserved, both, I was sure, full of love just waiting to be brought to the surface. A niggling voice inside my head suggested that Linda wasn't the obvious candidate for stepmother of two small children under ten, but I brushed it aside.

"I think Dave should come to the movies with us," Linda was saying. "Cheer him up, don't you think?"

I agreed enthusiastically.

"Great," Dave said. "I'll just call my mother and ask her to cope with the kids tonight. Come and collect me when you're ready to leave. You know, Loring's death is going to mean we're going to have to hire someone to take over his class. I'd better have a talk with Rob about that."

Linda looked at her watch. "And I'd better call Anna and let her know what's happened. She should be back by now."

I went and sat in my office. It was the one that belonged to the member of the department who was on a sabbatical and was decidedly unrestful, since its usual occupant was obviously an enthusiastic collector of rather inferior modern art—all swirling reds and yellows with strange shapes that almost made sense, but mostly didn't, so that they caught the eye and niggled away at the mind without ever being resolved. I sat with my back to the most intrusive of these paintings and tried to think. I hardly felt I could come right out and ask Sam where she had been on the night of the concert when Max Loring was murdered, but she'd certainly had a motive for killing him. And, in a way, a sort of motive for killing Carl as well. After all, he had tried to get her thrown out of Wilmot and she was almost obsessionally keen to finish her master's degree—to prove, I suppose, that she was not just some pretty girl on the make, but a woman of proven intellectual achievement. Carl hadn't succeeded, but it wasn't for want of trying. But was Sam so vindictive that she had borne a strong enough grudge to lead to murder? They say that the first murder is the difficult one; perhaps, after killing Max, the murder of his brother wouldn't seem so hard.

And, really, who *would* have had a motive for killing both Lorings? I considered my only other suspect, Walter Cleveland. *He* would have had no obvious reason to kill Carl, and even if Carl had somehow found out that Cleveland had murdered his brother and had to be silenced, then surely *someone* would have noticed a visitor as unusual and important as Cleveland wandering round the corridors. It was possible that Mike would turn up some other suspect we none of us knew about, someone outside the department altogether. What about Carl's boyfriend, the actor that Anna had mentioned? There could well be several such young men that we knew nothing about. . . . The picture on the wall opposite caught my eye relentlessly. Was that peculiar triangular shape a witch's hat and, if so, perhaps what I had taken for a careless brushstroke *might* just be a broomstick. I abandoned my confused thoughts on Carl Loring's murder and gave myself up to this new problem.

10

"So that's two cheeseburgers, two quarter-pounders—one without relish—and fries and coffee for everyone, okay?" Anna made her way to the counter, and Linda, Dave, and I sat at a plastic-topped table as far away from the piped music as we could.

Dave showed a tendency to want to discuss new schedules with Linda, but she said firmly, "No shop—tonight is happy time."

"Actually," Dave said, "I hate to say this, and I could only say it to you, but having Loring out of the way is enjoyment enough in itself!"

And certainly we all seemed to have a feeling of euphoria. Even Anna, who wasn't involved in the department's affairs like the rest of us, caught the mood, and if our liveliness that evening had a slight edge of hysteria, then our enjoyment was none the less for that. The movie, which matched our mood, was a romantic comedy of the kind (I couldn't help thinking, in my middle-aged way)

Cary Grant and Katharine Hepburn used to do rather better, but cheerful and agreeable so that when Linda, Anna, and I got back home, we were in high spirits.

"There's some ice cream in the freezer and that coffee cake left from yesterday if anyone wants some," Anna said.

"Great," Linda enthused, "I'm starving. What about you, Sheila?"

"Yes, please," I said. "It would round off the evening very well. Dave is nice, isn't he?" I continued.

"He's a great guy." Linda's head was inside the freezer so I couldn't see her face. "I don't know how I'd have hung on sometimes without his support. All that business with Loring, that started when Dave took my side in one of our departmental fights."

She emerged with two cartons. "Strawberry or vanilla with chocolate fudge?"

"Well, all that's over now," Anna said. "You might even begin to enjoy your work again."

"Well, now that he's gone," Linda said thoughtfully, "the focus of opposition will be gone, too, if you see what I mean. Nora O'Brien and the egregious Rick haven't got the pull with Rob Huron that Loring had. I feel Huron was always a bit afraid of Loring."

"Goodness!" I exclaimed. "There's an idea! Perhaps Loring had some kind of *hold* over Rob; perhaps he was blackmailing him! Now that would be a motive for murder!"

"Yes," Linda said doubtfully, cutting a slice of cake, "but can you see Rob killing anyone? He's so indecisive he'd have had that knife in the air so long while he was trying to make up his mind that Loring would have simply taken it away from him! It would have been Hamlet all over again!"

"Oh, dear, I'm afraid you're right," I agreed. "Reluctant as I am to lose a perfectly good suspect that none of us likes, I have to agree. Which, I'm afraid, only leaves us with Sam."

"Oh, no!" Anna protested.

"Well," I said, "she does have a sort of motive for both murders, and she hasn't an alibi for today."

I told them my theory about the invitation card and how she might have slipped into the institute.

"No," Anna said flatly. "I'm sure I didn't leave my bag around in the common room that day."

But there was something in her voice, a note of uncertainty, that made me wonder if she couldn't admit, even to herself, that such a thing might have happened.

"By the way," I asked Linda, "did you hear from Gina eventually?"

"No," she replied, "I didn't. I hope she shows up tomorrow, otherwise I'll have to go around to her apartment and see what's happened. I'm sure there's something wrong."

* * *

The Thai restaurant was very dark, lit only by candles whose precarious light was almost extinguished every time the door was opened to admit another customer.

"I don't think I can see to read the menu," I said to Mike. "You'll have to tell me what to order."

"Well now," he said. "There's Kai Tom Kah—that's chicken with coconut milk and lemon grass, among other things—or Tom Yam Kung, which is lobster done the same way, or there's Kaeng Pheet Kai, a sort of chicken curry, but I'd better warn you, that's pretty hot, a lot of chilies."

"Oh, the lobster thing, I think. It sounds delicious," I replied, rather taken aback by this expertise. "Do you cook yourself?"

"I've had to, I guess. So I kind of got interested. It's very relaxing. When I'm home, that is. Sometimes, after a really hard day, the temptation just to say what the hell and order a pizza is very strong, but usually I rustle up something. I guess I don't have to tell you that I'm fond of my food." He indicated his bulky waistline. "Too fond, perhaps! Julia Child is my favorite bedtime reading. How about you?"

"Oh, yes," I replied enthusiastically. "I cook myself what are known as proper meals, even when Michael's not at home. Like you, I find cooking therapeutic. If a book isn't going well or I'm bogged down in a mass of material and it all seems too much, then I go into the kitchen and cook something. Very rich fruitcakes are particularly soothing. I think it's something to do with having to measure out so many ingredients!"

"Did you find it very difficult, being alone," Mike inquired, "after your husband died, when your son was away?"

"Yes," I said. "Yes, it was very bad. Peter had been ill for a long time, and I knew it *would* happen, but somehow you're never really prepared; it still comes as a terrible shock. And my mother had died just before; I simply felt my world had fallen apart. If it hadn't been for Michael . . ."

I was glad the restaurant was so dark as the tears came into my eyes, as they always do when I think of that time. I blinked a bit to clear them away and went on, "You get used to it, of course. Life goes on, the raw tissue heals, but you always carry the scar."

The food arrived: lots of little dishes with unfamiliar things in them.

"This lobster thing's very good," I said.

We devoted our attention to the variety of food for a little while and then I continued, "Actually, to lose someone by death is probably more bearable, in some ways, than going through a divorce. I mean, if you still care very much for the other person, thinking of them still being *there*, perhaps with someone else . . ."

"Yes," Mike said, "I guess it's a different kind of hurt. And there's the sense of failure, too. You feel if only you'd done something different, been a different person . . ."

"And you lost your daughter, too. That was hard. I'm so lucky to have Michael. Even when he leaves home, he'll still be—what's the phrase you all use over here?—*there* for me. I still have that."

"Is that enough?" he asked. "I mean," he continued tentatively, "have you ever thought about marrying again?"

Even in the dimly lit restaurant I was very aware of his gaze.

"No," I said firmly, "I'd never do that. When you've had one really marvelous marriage, then that's it. There'd be no point somehow."

We sat in silence for a moment, unspoken words hanging between us. I think we both knew that if nothing were said on either side, then the situation would remain tenable. We could continue a pleasant, light relationship, maintain the fiction that there were no deeper feelings involved. I still found it strange that Mike should have these feelings on so short an acquaintance. I was flattered, in a way, as any woman might be, but embarrassed and uneasy, not quite sure how to handle the situation.

"That guy Dave Hunter," Mike said suddenly, "he's changed his story."

"What!"

"Now he says he was in the common room at ten-fifteen." Mike spooned some lime sauce from the dish in front of him onto his curry.

"But, goodness," I said, relief that we were now on safer ground conversationally, making me react more strongly than the information might seem to warrant. "That's really cutting things a bit fine. I mean, there were people in there almost up to ten o'clock, when most of them had classes. Would there have been *time* for someone to have met Loring in the common room and kill him like that?"

"Practically speaking, I guess"—Mike spoke slowly—"there would have been—that is, if it was premeditated and not the result of some sort of conversation or quarrel. One thing I did learn: Carl Loring went into the common room just before ten o'clock. Someone called Johnson told me he was the last to leave, and just as he was going, Carl Loring came in. They exchanged a few words about some business Loring had been to see this guy Huron about—something to do with a committee—and Johnson went on his way."

"So he must have been the last person to see Loring alive," I said. "Except for the murderer, I suppose. Does Rick Johnson have an alibi?"

"Yes, he was giving some sort of movie show in the little theater," he replied. "There were quite a few students there."

"I still can't get over anyone *teaching* film," I said irrelevantly. "So I suppose that lets him out. Anyway, he was rather a Loring supporter, especially now that there was this idea of reequipping the theater, all those plans. I suppose," I said regretfully, "we really can't pin Max Loring's murder on his brother now?"

"Too soon to say yet if the murders were done by the same person." Mike poured some more water onto the mound of ice in my glass. "Max Loring was shot; his brother was knifed. Different methods. It could be that Carl Loring killed his brother—for money, perhaps, though there may be other family reasons we haven't found yet. Then someone seized the opportunity to kill Carl, someone who had a really sound alibi for Max's murder who might hope we'd think the murders were both done by the same person."

"Or," I said excitedly, "someone like Walter Cleveland, who had a motive for murdering Max Loring, might have killed *him*, and then someone who wasn't anywhere near the institute that night could have killed Carl for totally different reasons."

"There's a lot of work to be done," Mike said. "We're only just at the beginning."

We all went about our business as usual at Wilmot. Most of us felt (guiltily) a sense of relief that now we could get on with things peacefully.

"Not having to look over our shoulders," Sara said, "to see if Loring is going to stab us in the back. Oh, my God! I shouldn't have said that, should I? But you know what I mean."

Gina telephoned Linda to say that she was ill.

"She was sick, in bed, when I called the other morning," Linda said. "She said she couldn't get to the phone in time. Some sort of virus. She hasn't been able to get down to the doctor's office yet."

"But surely he's been to visit her?" I said. "If she's feeling so bad."

"This is Allenbrook," Linda said, "not Taviscombe. Here you're either well enough to go to see the doctor, or else you're in the hospital. No one makes house calls."

"But that's *awful!*" I said, thinking of my own splendid Dr. Macdonald. "I couldn't have survived Michael's childhood—tonsilitis, mumps, scarlet fever, you name it, he had it, all usually flaring up at eleven o'clock at night!—if my doctor hadn't visited. Shouldn't one of us go round and see how Gina is? I mean, she might need medicines or something."

"I did offer," Linda replied, "but she said she had everything she needed and just wanted to stay in bed for a bit."

"Oh, well," I said, "perhaps that's why she's been so odd lately. She must have been sickening for this."

The next morning I was going through some class papers in my room at Wilmot when the fluorescent light over my desk went. Although I had a rather fancy anglepoise lamp that looked like some strange prehistoric bird, there wasn't really room for it on my desk when I had my papers all spread out. Reluctantly I got to my feet and went in search of one of the janitors.

There were two janitors who looked after the department building: Ben, who was young, cheerful, and obliging, and Gus, who was old, disagreeable, and unhelpful. There was no sign of Ben, but I finally found Gus in the furnace room, where he was engaged in some mysterious ploy that necessitated his moving a pile of boxes from one side of the extensive space to the other. I greeted him with that bright, false jollity I always find myself employing when I want to propitiate people.

"I wonder," I said, "if you could be very kind and replace the fluorescent light in my room. I'm afraid it's too high up for me to manage it myself," I went on, as if such a course of action on my part were possible, though both of us knew that it wasn't.

Gus paused in his manhandling of a particularly large box. "I got all this to do," he said sourly, "and no help. That Ben, he's off somewhere. I shouldn't be doing heavy work like this here. Due to retire next year. I'm an old man. It ain't right I should be hauling boxes at my age. . . ."

He subsided into muttering, and I tried again.

"Well, perhaps if you came and changed the light for me now, by the time you'd done that, Ben would be back and could help you with these."

He paused and considered this. "Nope," he said. "These here boxes got to be shifted right away. That's what they said, right away."

"Oh, dear," I said helplessly, "what am I going to do?"

He ignored this feminine appeal with an ease, no doubt, born of practice and went back to his boxes.

"You don't know where Ben is, then?" I asked.

He regarded me scornfully. "If I'd a known where Ben was, I'd a had him here helping me with this."

"Yes, of course," I replied.

I looked about me. The furnace room was a cavernous place with pipes running round the walls and an enormous heating apparatus rearing up at one end, like some tribal god. Several doors led out from this space, and I suddenly thought of something.

"Are all these doors always locked?" I asked.

He looked up from his task and said laconically, "Should be."

"Were they locked last Monday?"

He straightened up. "You mean the day that guy was killed?"

"Yes," I said, noting that I seemed to have caught his attention at last. "I gather they were locked that day."

"Who says they was locked?" he asked truculently.

"Well," I replied, slightly taken aback by his manner, "I think Professor Huron told the police—"

He gave a snort of disgust. "They'd no business asking *him* about them doors. *He* wouldn't know if they was locked or open. He'd a *said* they was locked, because that's what they was supposed to be and *he* ain't ever going to admit things round here ain't perfect all the time."

From the heavily accented references to Rob Huron I deduced that Gus shared the general view of the department about their chair.

"If they'd a come to *me*," Gus went on, "I'd a told them. But no," he continued with heavy irony, "they wouldn't ask nobody who *knows* what goes on in this place."

"So the doors *weren't* locked that day?" I asked. "Not the one leading to the common room kitchen, for instance?"

"Nope. Couldn't be. Not when that Ben"—he brought out the name of his hated rival triumphantly—"broke the lock and it ain't been fixed yet."

"I see," I replied. "And what about this main door here?"

"Can't keep it locked all the time," he said defensively. "When you're in and out all day, you can't go off getting the key every goddamn time you want to move some *boxes*"—he scowled at the pile in front of him—"and junk like that."

"No, of course not," I said soothingly.

"You tell me," he demanded, "how I'm going to be in and out with *boxes* and stuff when I got to go and fetch the key every five minutes?"

"No," I said, "certainly not. You're absolutely right."

"What *he* don't understand," Gus went on remorselessly, "is that I ain't got but one pair of hands."

He turned back to the boxes again, and feeling myself dismissed, I went away to look for Ben.

"So you see," I said to Linda that evening as we washed up after supper, "someone could easily have got through that door from the furnace room into the kitchen without being seen. They wouldn't have had to go through the department as such at all. So it could have been *anyone*!"

"Well, I know Loring was pretty unpopular," Linda said wryly, "but I don't think—do you?— someone just came in off the street and murdered him."

"Idiot!" I said. "You know what I mean. It

doesn't actually have to be someone in the *department*. It could have been—oh, someone from the institute, perhaps, who had a reason for killing Max Loring and Carl found out somehow and so whoever it was crept in and killed him to keep him quiet."

"Still," Linda said, scraping away at the baked bits of lasagne that still clung to one of the dishes, "it would have had to be someone who knew Wilmot fairly well. Otherwise how would they know about the door from the kitchen to the furnace room?"

"Well, yes. I suppose so, but it would open up the field of suspects, wouldn't it?"

"Are you going to call your friend Mike and tell him?" Linda inquired.

"Oh, dear, I hadn't thought of that. I suppose I better had."

"Well, he ought to know," she said reasonably.

"Well, hello!" Mike sounded pleased when I rang.

"I've just found out something you ought to know," I said, and told him what I had gleaned from Gus. "He's right, of course. Rob Huron never would admit that anything wasn't as it should be, so he'd automatically say that the doors were locked without actually *checking* that they were."

"Yes, well, I guess I slipped up there," Mike

said. "I should have checked for myself. Thanks, Sheila, that was neatly done!"

"But it does open up the field of suspects, don't you think?" I asked.

"And even more important," he said thoughtfully, "it helps with the timing. It's been bothering me how the murderer could have been in and out so quickly if that guy Hunter was telling me the truth, and it would be an odd kind of thing to lie about because it would increase suspicion on him. Though I still can't figure out why he changed his story."

"You mean," I exclaimed, "that the murderer might still have been in the kitchen when Dave went into the common room?"

"I'd think that was quite likely," he replied.

"Goodness!" I said. "It must have been quite a scary moment for him."

"Or her," Mike suggested.

"Well, yes, I suppose so," I said. "So he—or she—came and went through the furnace room door. Come to think of it, nobody would notice anyone going in and out of the furnace room, it's pretty well off the beaten track at Wilmot, and I've got a strong suspicion that Gus and Ben aren't in there very much. Ben, I know, likes to be around the department chatting to anyone who'll listen, and Gus spends quite a lot of time in a sort of little shack by the parking lot, doing goodness knows what!"

Mike laughed. "For a newcomer to Wilmot you've certainly got most people pretty well figured out."

"You don't really suspect Dave Hunter, do you?" I asked. "I mean, I know it's the classic 'last person to see the victim alive' situation, but Dave wouldn't have a real motive."

"It seemed to me," Mike said, "that his hatred of this Loring guy was rather more than just colleagues bickering. Wasn't there a real chance that he might lose his job?"

"No, Dave had tenure," I replied. "Loring couldn't get him dismissed."

"But there was real bad blood between them," Mike persisted. "When he spoke to me, he got pretty well worked up about various issues they'd fought about."

"Oh, well," I said quickly, "Dave does get carried away sometimes."

"A constant friction, going on for some time, especially at a bad time for him, when he'd just lost his wife. People can go to pieces at a time like that." Mike spoke quietly and with feeling. "You don't think too straight when something like that happens; you don't have a sense of proportion. Sometimes you just have to lash out at whatever seems to be a source of aggravation."

"It still doesn't seem enough of a motive for murder," I said doubtfully.

"A really little thing can lead to murder," Mike

said. "You'd be surprised. What did surprise me with Hunter," he went on, "was the way he almost wanted to draw suspicion to himself. Now that really did get me wondering."

"You mean," I said curiously, "as if he wanted to draw it away from another person? But why should he want to do that?"

"Well," he said, "the obvious reason would be that he was trying to protect someone."

"Someone he might have thought had actually *done* the murder, you mean?" I asked.

"It has been known."

"Well," I said roundly, "I can't think of anyone in the department he felt *that* strongly about!"

But I knew very well who Dave might be wanting to protect, and that was something I had no wish to think about too deeply.

11

"I must remember to order a cake from Schmidt's," Linda said. "It's a sort of *thing*, when it's your birthday, to provide cake for the department. Silly, really, but we all do it."

"Even Loring?" I asked.

"Oh, yes"—she laughed—"usually something *very* fancy, so that he could make a show, of course."

"Don't order one," I said on a sudden impulse. "Let me make one instead. How would you like a rich fruitcake? A Dundee, perhaps?"

"Wow!" Linda said. "A genuine Malory cake, like those you used to give me in Taviscombe?"

"If you'd like it," I replied. "I think perhaps I'd better make two, while I'm about it, so's there's enough to go round. I don't suppose," I went on, "you have any sort of cake tin for me to bake it in. I thought not. Well, I shall buy one—no, two—and leave them with you in the hope that one day you'll take up cakemaking yourself. It's highly therapeutic and probably much better for you than jogging. I don't believe anyone ever died of a heart attack while making a cake!"

I had a free morning, so I thought I'd go down to the local supermarket and get the ingredients. I love American supermarkets, not just because the products on the shelves are so rich and strange, but because the atmosphere and, indeed, the whole shopping ethos are quite different. As I said to Anna once, when we were in D'Agostino's in Brooklyn, if I told people in Taviscombe that I was buying an enormous T-bone steak at ten o'clock on a Sunday night, they simply wouldn't believe me!

I was looking with my usual feeling of wonderment and awe at the immense slabs of meat that seemed to make up a normal American portion, when a voice behind me said, "Somebody else doing the shopping, too!"

It was Dave Hunter.

"That's some basketful you have there," he said. "Can I give you a hand?"

"No, I'm fine," I said. "I think the entire female population of England, over the age of fifty, has one arm longer than the other from carrying heavy shopping baskets. It's all those years we spent going from shop to shop on foot before we had supermarkets!"

"I'm just picking up some ground beef for the kids," Dave said. "My mother's out tonight, and hamburgers are about the limit of my culinary capacity."

We made our way to the checkout, and as our things were being packed away in those lovely strong brown paper bags, I said, "Now I must go and find some sort of tin to bake all this in. I suppose Katy's Kitchen will have one. I wonder," I went on tentatively, "have you got a spare half hour? Do you feel like having a coffee? There's something I'd like to talk to you about."

Dave looked slightly surprised at this request but said agreeably enough, "Sure, I'd like that."

As we sat down in the little café and ordered our coffee, he said, "This is nice, I don't think I've ever been here before. I just seem to gravitate to the Blue Moon Diner like the rest of the department."

"Oh, I love that, too," I said. "It's just like the movies. So many of our ideas of America, all the things we expect to find, are colored by what we saw in films way back in our youth!"

We conversed politely for a while about the differences between England and America, but I could see that he was curious to know why I had asked him to come. The trouble was, now that I was actually face-to-face with Dave Hunter, it seemed increasingly difficult to find the words to ask him the questions that were in my mind.

"They have very good doughnuts here—" I was saying when he interrupted me.

"What exactly did you want to talk about?" he asked.

"Oh, dear," I said, "this is rather difficult!"

He gave me a reassuring smile. "It's okay," he said. "I'm quite approachable. I don't bark, bite, or take offense."

I finished off the remains of my coffee to give me confidence and plunged in. "It's about what you told the police," I said, "about finding Loring—Well, not that exactly. It's changing your mind and saying that you were in the common room at about ten-fifteen."

The smile faded from his face. "What's so strange about that?" he replied. "I made a mistake about the time when I first spoke to the lieutenant. When I thought about it later, I realized I was there earlier than I'd said."

"With everyone else going off to their classes at ten o'clock," I said, "leaving Loring behind, and you going into the common room at ten-fifteen—well, that doesn't leave a lot of *time* for the murder to be committed. You must have known that telling Lieutenant Landis you were there just fifteen minutes after Loring was left alone must make you the prime suspect."

He was fiddling with his coffee cup and didn't meet my eye.

"I didn't murder him," he said eventually. "I assure you, I didn't murder Loring."

"No one in their right mind would ever think you had!" I said briskly.

This had the effect of bringing his head up. His gray eyes looked anxious behind the heavy-rimmed glasses.

"I do have a sort of motive," he said. "And I really *hated* Loring. I expect the lieutenant will have latched on to that."

"It's not the sort of motive that would really stand up in court, now is it? A lot of academic squabbles! And as for hating Loring, well, you're only one among many!"

We sat in silence for a moment. Then I said, "It seems to me, and I think it may have occurred to the lieutenant as well, that you're trying to shield someone."

"No!" The word was almost jerked from him.

"And," I continued, "it seems to me that the only person in the department you might want to shield is Linda."

He gave a little laugh. "Is it that obvious?" he said ruefully.

"Well, I am a very old friend," I said, "and I notice things."

"Yes, well, Linda has been a real lifeline for me since Elaine died. I guess I sort of found myself caring for her more and more, you know how it is? I know she doesn't feel the same way about me—"

"Oh, she's very fond of you," I said quickly, "really devoted."

"I'm a dear friend," Dave said sadly, "nothing more. You know Linda, I don't think she's ever felt much more than friendship for anyone—except this guy—

"You mean the one in Oxford, David Hamble?" I said. "He was nice, but I always felt it was like an experiment, on Linda's side, anyhow. Something she knew wasn't going to last."

"No," he said, "I was thinking of someone else."

"Really?" I looked at him in astonishment. "I'd no idea!"

"It was last year," he said. "A mature student. Doug Chapman. She was supervising his doctoral thesis—Tennyson, I forget the exact title. He was a remarkable man, had been all over the world, lived in the Kalahari among the Bushmen for a time, up and down mountains in the Himalayas, that sort of thing. He'd been injured, thrown from a horse in South America somewhere; he'd lost an arm and had some sort of metal plate in his head, but great company, lively and very entertaining. We all liked him."

"He sounds almost too good to be true, a real storybook hero!" I said.

"He was certainly larger than life," Dave agreed.

"So what on earth was he doing at Wilmot, working on Tennyson, of all people?" I asked.

"He said he'd turned to literature when he was

in the desert. He had a really fine brain; I guess he was the sort of person who could have mastered anything he set his mind to. But he was broke, he said, and had to earn some sort of living, not really easy with his disabilities. He'd been teaching part-time at a state college in Tennessee, and he needed his doctorate for the full-time job they wanted to give him."

"And you think Linda felt something special for this Doug?" I asked.

"They were very close, away from Wilmot as well as in the department," Dave replied. "Anna was away in Italy just then, so I guess she was glad of the company, but it wasn't just that: She was really . . . infatuated." He brought out the word with difficulty.

"So what happened?" I asked. "Where's this man now?"

"Tennessee, I guess. He got the job."

"But Linda?" I asked.

Dave took off his glasses and polished them with a tissue. "Just before he went," he said, "they split up, never saw each other again. It hit her pretty hard."

"But why did they break up?" I demanded.

"You'd have to ask her that."

I looked at him sharply, but he met my gaze steadily.

"Dave," I said after a moment, "has all this

something to do with why you were trying to shield Linda?"

He was silent for a while and then, as if he had suddenly come to a decision, he said, "I suppose I'd better tell you. You're a good friend to Linda, I know, I believe I can trust you, and I do need to tell someone."

He rested his elbows on the table and leaned towards me.

"I was just turning into the corridor," he said quietly. "That was around ten-thirty, when I saw Linda coming out of the common room. She turned the other way and didn't see me. When I first spoke to the lieutenant, I hadn't really taken in the timing of the murder, and I didn't realize that Linda hadn't told him she'd been in the common room then. No one else went into that room after I did, and I found the body ten minutes later."

"There's no way," I said firmly, "that Linda could murder anyone! Anyway, she had no motive. Just the usual academic rows with Loring that everyone else had."

Dave was silent, and I said sharply, "That *was* all, wasn't it?"

"Honestly, Sheila, I can't say anything," he said wretchedly. "You'll have to ask Linda."

"You mean there was something, but surely . . ."

"I can't say any more," he repeated. "I've probably said too much already."

"I'm glad you did," I said. "Linda is one of my dearest friends, and I can't believe she'd kill anyone, whatever sort of motive you may think she has. Besides," I suddenly realized, "the fact that you saw no one else in the common room isn't conclusive! No, I'm not mad, listen. The door from the kitchen into the furnace room *wasn't* locked that day, so the murderer could have escaped that way while you were actually in the common room."

Dave looked startled. "You mean the murderer might have been in the kitchen while . . ."

"Think hard," I urged him. "Did you hear anything?"

He shook his head. "Nothing I can remember."

"But if there *was* someone in the kitchen, they must have heard you coming into the common room," I said.

"I guess so," he replied.

"Anyway," I went on, "it does mean that although Linda *seems* to have been the last person in the common room before you found Loring, there's still a good possibility that the murderer was still in the kitchen with the body when you went in."

He buried his head in his hands. "I'm all mixed up now," he said. "You may be right about the murderer escaping through the furnace room door, but that still doesn't explain why Linda hasn't said that she was in the common room then."

"She may just have put her head round the door," I said, "not actually gone in. She was looking for Gina, remember?"

There was a short silence, and then I said, "I'll have a word with Linda. Perhaps there's a perfectly simple explanation."

"Maybe." Dave looked at his watch. "Hell, I've got a class in half an hour. I've got to go. Let me know how things go with Linda, will you? And thank you, Sheila. I feel a whole lot better now that I've spoken to you."

He went away, and I drifted off to buy the baking tins, but now, I realized, I had something else to hide from Mike, and that made me feel very uncomfortable.

Linda didn't get back until about seven o'clock.

"Hey!" she cried as she came into the kitchen. "Will you look at those cakes!"

"Are they all right?" I asked. "Do you think there'll be enough to go round?"

"They're great," she said enthusiastically. "And what's all this? You've got supper, too?"

"Oh, well, while the oven was on, I thought I'd make us a shepherd's pie."

"A shame Anna's gone back to New York," Linda said. "She adores your shepherd's pie."

"Made with real shepherd!" we both chorused, echoing an old joke.

I had thrown myself into an orgy of cooking that afternoon to try and sort out my thoughts and feelings about Loring's death and Linda's possible part in it. But I had come to no sort of rational conclusion, my mind squirreling around as I went through the well-worn ritual of creaming the butter and sugar, beating the eggs, and greasing the tins. Now Tiger, attracted by the smell of cooking, came into the kitchen and began weaving round my legs demanding food.

As I took his tin out of the fridge I summoned up my resolution and said to Linda, "I had coffee with Dave today. I wanted to ask him why he changed his story and told Mike he was in the common room at ten-fifteen. I mean, he couldn't have been, could he?"

Linda paused in the act of unscrewing a bottle of tonic water. "What do you mean?" she asked.

"Well . . ." I bent my head over Tiger's tin, easing the cat food out onto the dish and carefully mashing it with a fork. "Well, Dave told me he saw you coming out of the common room at ten-thirty, though apparently you didn't see him. *That's* why he changed his story. He was protecting you."

Linda sat down suddenly. "Oh, God!" she said. "What a mess!"

I put Tiger's food down on the floor and went

and sat beside her. "Linda," I said softly, "my dear, what's going on? Please tell me."

"I need a drink," she said, and poured two large gin and tonics. "Here," she said, and pushed one towards me. "Yes, I was there around then."

"Looking for Gina?" I asked.

"Yes." She'd finished her drink and was pouring another. "Good old Dave, he certainly is one hell of a guy, don't you think?"

"He's really devoted to you," I said.

"Yeah—that's a shame, too." She turned her tumbler round and round, seemingly totally absorbed in the movement of the liquid against the glass.

"Why didn't you tell anyone you'd been in the common room?" I ventured at last.

"You mean your friend Mike?"

"Well, yes. Or me or Dave, or any of your friends at least."

"I was scared, I guess," she said. "I *really* wanted Loring dead, you know. I had one hell of a motive."

"All that departmental bickering?" I exclaimed. "No way is that a real motive for murder!"

"Oh, there was something a lot more compelling than all that stuff," Linda said with a little laugh. "Dave knew about it. That's why he tried to cover up for me."

"Can you tell me about it?" I asked gently.

"What about Mike?" she said, looking at me

quizzically. "Won't you feel obliged to pass it on? I mean, you are supposed to be helping him."

"For God's sake, Linda," I cried, "you're my friend, my very dear friend. How can you think for one *moment* that I'd pass anything on that might hurt you in any way!"

She smiled and laid her hand briefly on my arm. "Sure," she said, "silly of me to ask. I guess I'm just finding it hard to tell you about something I bitterly regret, about making a fool of myself . . ."

"Dave told me," I said tentatively, "a bit about someone called Doug Chapman. Has all this anything to do with him?"

Tiger, having finished his food, jumped up onto the table and rubbed his head against her arm. Linda picked up the cat and held him close for a moment. Then she put him down on the floor and said, "Sure, it has. I don't really know where to begin. Dave probably told you a little bit about Doug. He really was something special. You've known me long enough to realize I'm not drawn to that sort of macho, outdoor hero type, so at first I was a little bit scornful. . . . I thought the literature bit was just an act, maybe what he thought was an easy way to get some sort of teaching job. But it was genuine, all right. His mind—oh, it was so *clear,* he just absorbed things and made them a part of himself, do you know what I mean? A sort of empathy that goes hand in hand with a clarity of critical judgment. It's a rare gift. I'd never met anyone like that before. Working with him on his thesis was—how can I put it?—*thrilling*. It was on Tennyson, did Dave tell you? Not exactly promising, you'd think, but he brought the man alive for me, the whole period, for that matter."

"That must have been wonderful!" I said softly.

Linda gave me a little, painful smile. "I guess I really made a fool of myself over that guy," she said.

"But why?" I asked. "Did he not feel the same way about you?"

"Oh, he said he did. Perhaps he really did, I don't know now. But then it was all so fantastic, something I never thought could happen for me. . . ."

She sat quietly for a moment, her thoughts far away; then she said briskly, "It didn't help, I suppose, that Anna was abroad; there was no one to tell me to think about what I was doing."

"But surely," I said, "if you were happy?"

"Fool's paradise," she said, and got up abruptly to pour another drink.

"So what *happened*?" I asked.

Linda came back slowly and sat down again beside me. I could feel the tension in her as she slowly sipped her drink. At last she said, "Doug had finished his doctoral thesis and handed it in to me. He'd never let me look at it before—not till it was done. It was brilliant, of course, as I knew it would be. There was just one thing, though. The main argument depended on one important piece of evidence, and"—her voice broke slightly—"he'd falsified it."

We were both silent. Then I said tentatively, "Are you sure?"

"Yes." She spoke very softly so that I had difficulty in hearing her. "Not many people would have known, but I'd seen the Benson papers, the ones that have just been released at Cambridge. There's a mass of material, not properly classified yet, but—well, ironic, isn't it?—that almost the one person in the States who *would* have known what he'd done had to be here at Wilmot, had to be me."

We were silent again. It's difficult to explain to nonacademic people, really, just how strongly one reacts to something like that. "For heaven's sake!" they say impatiently. "What does it matter? It's all ancient history anyway, so who cares?" But it *does* matter, in an almost emotional way. When you come up against something like that you get a real feeling of pain and—it sounds silly—of loss.

"Oh, Linda," I said, "how awful."

She shook her head. "That wasn't the *really* awful thing," she said.

"What happened?" I asked. "What did he say when you confronted him with it?"

Linda looked at me, her eyes level with mine, so that I was somehow unable to look away.

"You did confront him?" I asked. "Didn't you?"

Her eyes filled with tears, and she turned her head away at last. "No," she said, "not at first, not then. I—I couldn't. It would have been a denial of all that wonderful time we'd had together, having to admit to myself that the person I cared so much about could have done something like that. And then, well, I was infatuated, I guess, and you don't think clearly when things are that way. I kind of closed my mind to it, wouldn't confront it, even in my thoughts. So the thesis went through, and Doug got his job."

She sat very still, her head bent now as if she couldn't look at me. I put my hand over hers.

"Poor Linda," I said, "my poor girl!"

Linda looked up and gave me a grateful smile. "It was only when he told me that the job had come through that I faced up to what I'd done, and even then I tried to make excuses: He was brilliant; he'd be a fine teacher, able to inspire his students as he'd inspired me. And then he was disabled; it might not be easy for him to get anything else. . . ."

Her voice trailed away. I knew how difficult it must have been for her, more than for most people. Linda had a fierce integrity, quick to condemn falseness in others. With herself she would have been—well, I could see the pain even now.

"And by then it was somehow too late. I couldn't say anything, it was something I'd have to live with. But quite suddenly I found I hated him. No, not hated, despised! He had so much going for him intellectually; he didn't need tricks like that. I found I couldn't bear to see him, even; I couldn't bear to think that I'd been"—she hesitated—"in love"—she brought out the phrase with difficulty—"with someone I couldn't respect."

She gave a short, bitter laugh. "I guess it was a judgment on me for getting involved with a student, however mature—wholly unprofessional, something I've always felt very strongly about. Maybe I'm old-fashioned, I don't know, but whenever it's happened here, I've said I think it's wrong. I certainly proved my point the hard way!"

She laughed again, the laugh turning into a sob.

I couldn't think what to say, so I simply pressed her hand again.

"Doug was puzzled, of course. He kept calling me and writing notes, asking what was up. Eventually I realized I had to see him. It wasn't a meeting I'd ever want to go through again."

"What did he say?" I asked.

She smiled wryly. "He said thank you. As if all I'd done was pass him the cream for his coffee. He didn't understand, you see. . . . I still have this picture of him standing there, smiling—that fantastic warm smile that made you feel he was giving you a part of himself, saying it meant so much to him and wasn't I great to do this thing for him, and he'd never forget . . . crap like that!"

Her voice broke, and the tears poured down her cheeks. I put my arm round her shoulder.

"Oh, Linda," I said, "you poor child!"

She found a tissue, wiped her eyes, and said, "Sorry, Sheila, I thought I was all over it. . . ."

"You don't get over something like that," I said, "not really."

"Yes, I guess so. I listened to him for a while, just to prove to myself, maybe, just how worthless and insensitive he really was. Then I told him how I felt."

"How did he react?" I asked curiously.

She laughed, the same bitter sound. "He couldn't see it; he simply didn't understand what I was making such a fuss about. He thought we could still be . . . friends. I think he felt it bound us together somehow. Conspirators, maybe, us against the world. He was that sort of person; he loved to be different, apart from the common herd.

"I told him I'd say nothing and sent him away. He still couldn't believe that part, couldn't believe that his charm wasn't proof against something he regarded as unimportant. Unimportant," she repeated. "He actually said that the two of us were more important than some lousy technicality."

"Oh, Linda," I repeated. I couldn't find anything else to say.

She got up from the table and said, "I'm having another of these. How about you?"

We sat for a while in silence staring at our drinks, and then Linda said, "He went away. I didn't see him again, and that should have been that—except for the knowledge of what I'd done, and that would be with me always."

"Should have been?" I asked.

"Yes. But it wasn't. The fool, the damned *fool,* wrote me a letter from Tennessee. He still wanted us to see each other; he hated to let anyone go. I guess it would have hurt his ego to feel he'd been rejected. Anyway, he wrote a letter. It was quite a letter, too, saying what wonderful times we'd had together, how much he thought we cared for each other, and—oh, God—thanking me again for condoning that false statement in his thesis!"

"Oh, dear," I said inadequately. "That must have been awful. It must have brought back all those memories!"

Linda gave me a wry smile. "It brought more than that," she said.

"What do you mean?" I asked.

"I must have left the letter in a folder or something like that because I lost it. In the department."

"Oh, dear," I said, "that was awkward."

"And who do you think found it?"

"Not Loring!" I exclaimed.

"Yes," she said, "Loring. The letter was in its envelope, but I knew there was no way he wouldn't have read it. Reading other people's mail would have come quite naturally to a creep like him. Especially when he saw it was from Doug. You can imagine the sort of gossip and speculation there'd been about us in the department!"

"So what happened?" I asked.

"He gave the letter back to me with that vile sneer of his. 'I think this belongs to you,' or some such phrase, looking at me under those eyelashes to see how I was taking it, you can imagine."

"I can't believe that was all," I said thoughtfully.

"Right." Linda laughed. "He knew he had me where he wanted me. All of this happened just before the summer vacation, so I knew this semester he'd use the information he had from that letter to make my life hell."

"Why didn't he just go to Rob Huron?" I asked. "And tell him what he'd found out?"

"That would have been too simple," Linda said bitterly. "He really wanted to make me suffer, slow, long-drawn out misery, never quite knowing when he might strike. That was Loring's way."

"And I suppose," I said, "he couldn't quite admit that he'd read your letter."

"Oh, I don't think he'd have found that a problem," Linda said. "He'd have said it was by accident, some crap like that."

"Did he ever say anything directly about it?" I asked.

"Nothing overt, just snide remarks and dark

hints, usually in meetings, so that I couldn't oppose him. And then he'd smile and say how *great* it was to have my cooperation. Sara and Ted Stern must have thought I'd become really *flaky* this semester! And the really vile thing," she continued, "is that it's somehow brought me down to his level of morality. I find—I found that almost the hardest thing of all."

Tiger, annoyed that we were absorbed in other things, jumped up on my lap and began to knead my skirt with his claws. I stroked his head until he settled more comfortably and asked, "Dave knew all about it?"

She nodded. "Just before you came. I was in my room, crying—I seem to have been doing a lot of crying lately—and he asked what was the matter. Normally I wouldn't have told him, but I'd just had a run-in with Loring on the policy committee and was feeling, oh, *despairing*—I just couldn't bear it any longer. I had to tell someone."

"Hadn't you told Anna?" I asked curiously.

"No, I knew it would upset and worry her. I couldn't do that."

"She told me how concerned she was about you," I said, "but she thought you were just overworking."

"Yes, well, Anna's always looked after me, been the big sister, especially since Dan died. I somehow couldn't add to all that. So I told Dave."

She leaned her elbows on the table and rested

her chin on her hands. "It was a mean thing to do, I guess, to put such a responsibility onto him, but you know Dave, he seems like a rock. How could I imagine he'd try to throw suspicion onto himself to divert it from me!"

"You know how he feels about you," I said.

"Yes," she said quietly, "and that makes it much worse."

"He knows how *you* feel," I said, "and that you'll never be more than good friends, though that is no small thing."

"I suppose I'd better go to your lieutenant and tell him I was in the common room at ten-thirty," Linda said.

"No, don't do that," I said quickly. "I really don't think Mike seriously considers Dave as a murderer, so honestly, there's no need. Anyway, there's another thing to be taken into account."

I told her about the unlocked door into the furnace room. "So the murderer could have been and gone while you were in the common room," I said. "Did you hear any sound in the kitchen?"

"No, nothing." She was positive. "Anyhow, I was only in there for a few minutes, looking for Gina."

I stroked Tiger mechanically, and he began to purr and dribble slightly. "It all happened in such a brief space of time," I said. "So it must have been premeditated, I mean, there was hardly *time* for a row to blow up and then a murder. . . . Still,"

I went on, "the fact remains that Loring is dead and your secret is safe. I mean, he wouldn't have told anyone else, would he?"

"Oh, no," she replied, "not Loring. He would always hug any tiny little secret to himself; it gave a him a feeling of power, I guess. And this was something really big!"

"Well then," I said, with a brightness I was far from feeling, "you're in the clear. You can get on with your llfe, all of you, free at last from that *incubus*!"

But I knew that even with the threat from Loring removed, Linda would never be at ease with herself again.

"Shall I put the shepherd's pie in the microwave?" I asked. "Are you ready to eat?"

"Great! That'll be a real treat." Linda echoed my false cheerfulness, but neither of us had much appetite, and Tiger was the only one who really cleared his plate.

12

After that evening I had the feeling that Linda was avoiding me. I suppose it was only natural that she should. What had happened with Doug Chapman had obviously been really traumatic for her. As I said, Linda has this fantastically high academic standard; that's why she had clashed with Loring so often. To have had to admit that she, of all people, had done something she would regard as thoroughly shameful must have been incredibly hard for her. I respected her feelings and tried to go out as much as possible.

I had a pleasant evening with the Sterns, an incredible dinner beginning with Susan Stern's clam chowder ("my mother came from New England; I'll give you her recipe") and followed by a delicious chicken dish, accompanied by *seven* vegetables ("do you like beet tops? they're full of iron") and Ted's special chili sauce ("he makes it every year, and every year it gets hotter").

I went to dinner with Dave and his children

(impeccably behaved—I remembered with dismay how tiresome Michael had been at a similar age) and was the recipient of his mother's hopes for his remarriage to "a nice girl who'd be a real mother to the children." It was clear that she didn't feel that Linda fulfilled this particular job description.

I paid a visit to Sara and Charles and admired again the skill and ingenuity that had gone into transforming the mill.

"Oh, sure, it's great *now*," Sara said, "but I can remember lying in bed one morning and seeing a saw coming up through the wooden floor where Charles had suddenly decided to put in a new circular staircase!"

I even spent an extraordinary day with Sam and Hal (and the cats, dogs, horses, and goats) on their farm, which was certainly unlike anything we would call a farm in the West Country, being more like a vast estate with Sam (wearing diamonds with her jeans and sneakers) apparently taking for granted the amazing luxury with which she was surrounded.

And then there was Mike. He telephoned quite often, with offers of dinner or the movies, and I usually managed to find some excuse to refuse. He was a nice man, easy to talk to, comfortable to be with, but I had a twofold reason for avoiding him. It was obvious from his conversation that he still hoped for a closer relationship than I wanted, and now, with Linda's story and Dave's false evidence whirling round and round in my head, I felt I couldn't really face him. Not that I had any doubts of Linda's innocence—or Dave's either, for that matter—but I was uncomfortable in the knowledge that I was withholding *evidence*, something I'd been brought up by my lawyer husband to regard as sacred!

I was standing one morning regarding with interest the statue to General Gibbon that stood in the main square of Allenbrook. It was a fine figure in Union uniform, sword in hand. I craned my head to read the lettering:

GENERAL JOHN GIBBON
1827–1896
erected by his men of the Iron Brigade
Pennsylvania remembers her sons.

"There are some," a voice behind me said, "who'll tell you he was born in Holmesburg and not Allenbrook, but we have always claimed him as a native son."

I turned round and saw Mike.

"I didn't know that you were a Civil War enthusiast," he said, smiling.

"Goodness! You startled me," I said in some confusion.

"Or are you regarding it simply as an example of local art?" he inquired.

"No," I replied, "as a matter of fact, I felt I ought to find out *something* about local battles and local heroes for Michael, who's very keen on that sort of thing."

"Oh, well," Mike said, gesturing toward the general, "you couldn't do better than Gibbon. He was at Manassas and Antietam and commanded a division at Fredericksburg, where he was wounded. He was wounded at Gettysburg, too, and fought at the Wilderness and Spotsylvania. All in all, he had quite a war."

"Goodness," I said, "you *are* an expert! You must tell me what books I should take back for Michael."

"Sure, I'll make you a list, but look, why don't I take you to one of the battlefields? You could take pictures."

"Well," I said reluctantly, "I don't know. . . ."

He looked at me quizzically. "Do I get the feeling that you're avoiding me?" he asked.

"No, of course not!" I replied quickly.

"Right," he said. "You'll come then?"

He smiled again, and I suddenly felt foolish, as if I'd been making a fuss about nothing.

"That would be lovely," I replied.

"I suppose I should take you to Gettysburg, but, no, if you don't mind a really early start, it's a long drive, way into Maryland?"

"No," I said, "I don't mind. Where are we going?"

"I'm going to take you to Antietam, that's the place that sort of sums the whole thing up for me. How about next Sunday? I'll call you about the time."

"Thank you, Mike," I said, "that's very kind of you. I'll look forward to it."

"Oh, by the way," he said as I turned to go, "you might be interested to know: It looks like Carl Loring could have killed his brother."

"Good heavens!" I exclaimed. "Has something new come up?"

"Yes—something new and rather surprising, though I haven't got all the details yet. I'll let you know on Sunday."

"So, if that's what happened," I said thoughtfully, "then you're looking for two murderers?"

"Could be," he replied. "Like I said, it depends on this new information."

I went on my way pondering what he had said. If Carl Loring had murdered his brother and the two deaths weren't connected, then it was most likely that *his* murderer was someone at Wilmot.

And another thing, this scenario seemed to let out Sam. After all, it was the letter from Max that had cast suspicion on her. Her motive for killing Carl was nowhere near as strong. Well, that was a relief anyway. I liked Sam, and I didn't want to think of her as a killer. But if not Sam, then who? Dave? Linda? Impossible to consider either of them in such a role. Perhaps I needed to step right back and see who else might have needed Carl Loring out of the way. He was such a loathsome creature he must have had a hold over other people besides Linda.

Suddenly it all seemed too complicated and exhausting, and I just wanted to give up and go home. I thought of my house at Taviscombe and the garden, of Michael and the animals and all my comfortable and familiar friends, and I wished passionately that I was back there with them, away from all this unpleasantness and confusion. . . . Away, too, from Mike and the possible embarrassment of that situation. For a moment I really wallowed in homesickness so that it was almost a physical pain.

You are an absolute *fool*, I told myself sternly. Why do you have to *get* yourself into situations like this? But then I thought of Linda and Anna and all the new friends I'd made in Allenbrook (yes, Mike as well) and how they'd enriched my life, as all experience, however tiresome or indeed disagreeable it might seem at the time, *does* enrich it. And I acknowledged, too, my curiosity, which so often seemed to involve me in strange and often awkward situations, would drive me on until I had found *some* sort of solution. I began to wonder what new information Mike had and was impatient for Sunday to hear what it was.

I had a conference with Sam that day. Now that

I felt she was no longer a suspect I was able to relax and enjoy the splendid eccentricities of her personality.

"I did so enjoy the day I spent with you and Hal," I said.

"It was great having you over," she replied. "I wanted you to see the animals because I know just how caring you are about them."

"Oh, they were gorgeous!" I said enthusiastically. "And the farm! It's so enormous!"

"It's a good size," Sam conceded, "though nothing like the ranch that Hal has in Wyoming. I guess that's where we'll finally end up when I've finished at Wilmot. I'm going to make Hal wind things up here and settle right down and breed horses."

"Is everything all right between you two?" I asked tentatively. "There was no problem about the letter from Max Loring?"

"No," she replied, "the lieutenant was very understanding, didn't want to make trouble for me and Hal. I saw him that day at Wilmot, right after you suggested it, and he said that unless anything else turned up, there was no reason why Hal should ever know about that letter. And now that Carl's dead I don't think anyone else knows about it. Except you, of course, and"—she turned her brilliant smile upon me—"I'm sure you wouldn't say anything to Hal!"

"As if!" I laughed. "I'm so glad, Sam, that it's all worked out okay."

"That lieutenant," she said, "he's nice. I thought, the first time I saw him, he was just a cop, you know, but there's a lot there. That lazy sort of way he has with him hides a good mind, if you ask me."

I wondered if Mike had quoted Shakespeare to her; certainly her looks might well inspire poetic flights! But I was interested that Sam, a connoisseur of men if ever there was one, had found something in Mike to impress her.

I turned my mind to my work, and the conference continued. As she was leaving, I asked if she had heard anything from Gina.

"That virus seems to be taking its time," I said. "Do you think she's all right?"

"I haven't heard from her," Sam said after a moment's hesitation. "I guess I ought to call her."

"It's been a while," I said. "I haven't seen her since the day before Carl Loring died. How about you?"

"No," Sam said, "I haven't seen her either."

I looked at her. "It's a very good job you haven't had to lie to Hal," I said. "You're a very bad liar."

She turned her head away from me as if to hide her face. "I don't know what you mean," she said.

"I had a feeling," I went on, "the day of the murder, when I asked you about Gina, that you weren't telling me the truth, and now I'm convinced of it. Come along, Sam, surely you can trust me?"

She was silent, and I wondered if I'd been too abrupt with her, and then she said, "No, you're right. I *did* see Gina that morning."

"How was she?" I asked. "Was she ill?"

"No," Sam said reluctantly, "at least not with a virus."

"What do you mean?"

She got up and began to walk about the room, as if by doing so she could somehow dissipate the distress she obviously felt. She came to a halt in front of one of the bookcases and with her back to me said, "I guess if you had to sum up the way she was in one word, you'd say she was distraught."

"Distraught!" I cried. "What on earth do you mean?"

Sam turned to face me. Her expression was troubled.

"She looked terrible," she said. "Ghastly pale, and those dark eyes, they were huge, big as saucers. She looked as if she hadn't slept. She'd been crying, and her face was a mess. It was awful to see her."

"What did she say?" I asked.

"She didn't make a lot of sense," Sam said evasively.

"But she said something," I persisted.

"Yes, well—oh, what the hell!" She sat down

suddenly in the chair opposite mine. "She was asking me if I'd seen Loring, said she'd got to find him and he wasn't in his room. She was kind of wild, sobbing and breathless. I tried to calm her down, asked her what was the matter. I took her into one of the classrooms that were empty. I didn't want anyone to see her looking like that."

"Did you find out what it was about?" I asked.

"Yeah, she finally told me." Sam sounded very subdued, quite unlike herself.

"What was it?" I asked.

She sat with her head bent down, seemingly absorbed by one of her bracelets, twisting it round and round on her wrist so that the gold caught the light.

"Sam," I said, "please tell me what she said. You know it's important."

There was silence for several minutes, and then she said at last, "It was Rebecca."

"Rebecca?"

"Yes, Rebecca Long—she used to be in the department, as assistant professor," Sam said.

"Of course, I remember now. Loring managed to get the department not to give her tenure, didn't he? But what did that have to do with Gina?"

"She and Rebecca were a couple, you know," Sam said. "They'd been together quite a while, way back, from the time Gina first came to Wilmot. When they threw Rebecca out, Gina wanted to go with her to Washington, but Rebecca made Gina promise to stay on here and finish her incompletes and her thesis. I guess Gina was living for the day when she could be with Rebecca again."

"I suppose that's why she's not been concentrating too well on her work," I said.

"Yeah, well," Sam went on, "she started off okay, really trying to do things well, for Rebecca's sake. But then things began to go kind of wrong. Rebecca couldn't get a good college job; she had to take a job teaching public school in one of those tough inner-city areas. It was really bad. I guess she tried not to let Gina know just how bad—the violence, the drugs, and stuff like that—but Gina was no fool. She could read between the lines, and she was really worried. . . ."

"Poor child," I said, "it must have been very difficult for her. Did she go and visit Rebecca in Washington?"

"No, Rebecca kept putting her off. Maybe she didn't want Gina to see how things were. Well, things went on for a while like that—they wrote to each other and talked on the telephone—then Rebecca stopped writing, and she didn't answer when Gina called. Gina got more and more worried, and finally she told me she just had to go to Washington to see what was happening. Then—" Sam broke off.

"Then?" I prompted her.

"Then, that day, the morning I saw her," Sam said, "she'd just had a call from the police in Washington."

"The police!"

"Yeah. Rebecca left a note for Gina. . . ."

"A note? What . . . ? Oh, no! How terrible."

"Rebecca had taken an overdose," Sam said slowly. "She'd been there three days before they found her."

"Oh, God, how awful! No wonder Gina was in such a state." I looked at Sam. "She was asking for Loring?"

"I guess she wanted to tell him about Rebecca," Sam said. "She'd have blamed him. . . ."

"Did she say anything about that?" I asked. "I mean, about Rebecca's death being Loring's fault?"

Sam nodded. "She was really wild, saying crazy things."

"Oh, dear," I said. "Well, I can understand why you didn't say anything about seeing her. Poor Gina, who knows what thoughts were going through her mind that morning?"

"What are you going to do?" Sam asked.

"I really don't know," I replied wearily. "I suppose I'd better go and see her. Where does she live?"

"Here." Sam tore a piece of paper off her pad and scribbled an address. "It's almost in the center of town, not far."

"Oh, yes." I looked at the paper. "I think I know where it is—one of those streets off Lafayette Avenue, just past the Moravian church, is that it?"

"I guess I should have gone myself, before now," Sam said. "I feel bad that I didn't."

"Never mind," I said. "I'll go this afternoon. I'm free after four o'clock."

Gina's apartment was in fact the ground floor of a small house, white clapboard, front porch, like all the others in the street. They were quite old and looked a little run-down. I rang the bell and waited. Next door a young woman was sweeping leaves from her porch while a little boy in a brightly checked lumber jacket and cap played with a small gray cat. After a while I rang again, and then, when there was still no reply, moved along the porch and looked in through the window. There was no sign of life, and I was just going to see if I could find a way round to the back when the woman next door came over.

"You looking for Gina?" she asked.

"Yes," I said. "I can't seem to make her hear. She's one of my students, and she hasn't been well. I've been a bit worried about her."

"She ain't there," the woman said. "She's gone away."

"Gone away?" I echoed stupidly.

"Yeah," she said. "A couple of days ago. Said

she had to go away for a while. Asked me to look after her cat."

"Do you know where she was going or how long she'll be away?" I asked.

"She didn't say." The woman regarded me curiously. "Say, you're English, aren't you?"

"Yes," I replied, a little taken aback.

"Thought so. My pa, he was in England in the war. Some place called Norfolk. Are you from around there?"

"No," I said, "I'm afraid not. But I have a friend who lives there, near Swaffham."

"Hey," she cried, "he used to talk about that! And a place called Nor-wich, do you know that?"

"Yes," I said, "it's a very beautiful city."

"Well, how about that," she said. "You want a cup of coffee?"

"That's very kind of you," I said. "That would be lovely."

She led me into her house, saying to the child, "You come right in with me, Johnny, I don't want you scattering those leaves just when I've raked them."

The little boy picked up the cat and thrust it towards me. "That's Minna," he said. "She's Gina's cat, but I get to play with her when Gina's not here."

I took the cat from him and stroked her soft gray fur.

"She's lovely," I said. "Is she allowed to come indoors?"

The woman laughed. "He's crazy about that cat. I don't mind it indoors—keeps him quiet, and it's a clean little thing."

I followed her into a bright, cheerfully decorated kitchen, and we sat round a wooden table, while she put a kettle on the stove.

"My name's Gerda," she said, "Gerda Schantz, and this is Johnny."

"I'm Sheila Malory," I replied.

She took a jar down from the shelf. "You want a cookie?"

I accepted one and looked round the kitchen.

"What beautiful plants," I said, looking at the profusion of greenery on the windowsills. "I've never seen such a gorgeous variegated ivy!"

The gray cat settled down on my lap and began to purr. The little boy standing beside me gently stroked her head.

We talked for a while about plants and gardens and about England and her father, and then I tried to bring the conversation back to Gina. "I've been worried about her," I said. "She hasn't been well."

"She's looked pretty bad for a while now," Gerda agreed. "Not that I've seen her much; she's stayed indoors. Then that morning she went away, I was real shocked to see her. She looked terrible, like she hadn't slept for days. Real bad!"

"Did she have any luggage with her?" I asked.

"Don't know. She just rang my bell and asked about the cat, and I said, sure I'd see to it, and she thanked me and drove away. I tell you, I didn't think she looked fit to be driving, but what can you say to people? They'd just think you was interfering."

"I know," I said. "It's very difficult. And that was two days ago?"

"Yeah," she replied. "I sure hope she was okay, but I guess if there'd been an accident, we'd have heard by now."

"I suppose so," I said.

I got up and put the cat into the little boy's arms. "Thank you so much for the coffee," I said, "and I've enjoyed talking to you so much."

"Anytime you're around here," she said, "call in."

I walked away slowly, trying to fit this new piece of information into the puzzle of Loring's death. Gina, distraught at Rebecca's death, had gone in search of Loring. For what? To vent her hurt and pain on the person she held responsible for all that she and Rebecca had suffered? That much was obvious. But had she found him, and if she had, how far had she gone to revenge them both?

I had wandered into the burial ground of the small Moravian church, a white wooden edifice surrounded by trees and a large grassy plot. At my feet were small rectangular markers, the gravestones of early settlers in the town.

"Lewis David De Schweinitz, died January 1834," I read.

"Thomas Pechtowappid, a Mohican, dep. Aug. 26th 1746."

"Charles Colvier, a Revolutionary Soldier, dep. November 1817."

The dead brown leaves blew across the grayish white flat stones. A squirrel ran down from one of the plane trees, now leafless, paused and looked at me for a moment, and went on its way. Everything was very peaceful. Here in this quiet place, sheltered by the bare branches of the trees reaching up into the pale late-afternoon sky, there was no sound of traffic or, indeed, of any human activity. I stood for a while, my mind empty of all thought, until the light began to fail, and I turned to go.

13

"I must say I don't like the sound of that." Linda's voice was worried. I'd just told her about Gina. "She must have been in a terrible state when she went off," she said. "She was really devoted to Rebecca, went through a bad time when she went to Washington, but she was trying so hard to do what Rebecca wanted: finish her incompletes and her thesis. . . ."

Linda paused while she set a bowl of salad on the table. "I mean," she continued, "if she'd been brooding about Rebecca, all by herself like that!"

"I know," I replied. "Both Sam and the woman who lives next door were appalled at how dreadful she looked. Distraught, Sam said."

"She might have been going to Washington to pick up Rebecca's stuff or something," Linda suggested. "That would have been upsetting."

"I suppose so. I wish I knew what we ought to do."

"Yes."

We ate our salad in silence; then Linda said, "Perhaps you ought to call your friend Mike and tell him."

"But, Linda, I can't!" I cried. "He'd be frightfully suspicious of her if he knew!"

"Yeah, I know," she said, "but if something's happened . . ."

"Oh, Lord! What a mess!" I pushed my plate to one side. "I suppose," I said, "I could just say we were worried about her, in general terms, I mean. I could say she was upset about Rebecca, but I don't have to tell him why Rebecca left and the motive that gave Gina for killing Loring."

"You could do that."

We talked round and round the possibilities until I said wearily, "We have to tell him."

I got to my feet and dialed Mike's home number.

"Hi!" he said. "What's happened? Can't you make it on Sunday?"

"Sunday?" I echoed stupidly. "Oh, no, that's all right. No, it's something else. I'm rather worried. . . ."

I told him about Rebecca's suicide and Gina's distress.

"She hasn't been in touch with Linda or me, or anyone at Wilmot for a while, and now she's gone off, and we don't know where. She was in a terrible state. I'm so afraid something might have happened. . . ."

"I see." Mike sounded thoughtful. "You don't happen to know the license number of her car, do you?"

"No, I'm sorry," I said.

"Never mind," he replied. "I can check that. The Washington police were in touch with her, you say? I'll see if she's contacted them. Don't worry, Sheila. I'll do what I can and let you know as soon as I've got any news."

"Thank you, Mike," I said. "I'm awfully sorry to bother you about this, but she was frightfully upset, and honestly, if she *had* just gone to Washington, I think she'd have told somebody, even if it was only her next-door neighbor."

"It's okay," he said. "I'm glad you called. I'll get back to you as soon as I can."

It was next morning that he called. I'd just finished a class and had started to read through some of the student papers when the phone rang.

"Sheila? It's Mike."

Something in the tone of his voice made me ask quickly, "Mike! What's happened?"

"I'm afraid it's bad news," he said. "One of my officers found her car in the forest at Cedar Creek Park."

"Her car?" I asked.

"I'm afraid she was in it," he said quietly. "She'd taken some pills."

"Oh, no! Poor Gina, how terrible!"

Somehow, I wasn't surprised. In a way it was what I'd been expecting, and yet, as Mike said the words, I was suddenly and shockingly brought face-to-face with the awful fact of her death.

There was a little silence, and then Mike said, "There's something else."

"What is it?" I asked.

"Can I come around?" he said hesitantly. "There's something I need to show you."

"Yes, of course," I replied. "When?"

"Can I come right away?"

"Yes, of course. I can stay on for as long as you like."

I got up and went along to Linda's room, but she was in class. I thought of leaving her a note to tell her about Gina, but I didn't. I knew how upset she'd be, so it only seemed right that I should tell her in person.

I went back to my own room and tried to settle to the class papers while I waited, but I couldn't concentrate. I couldn't banish from my mind the picture of Gina slumped over the wheel of her car, alone, somewhere in the forest.

There was a tap on the door, and Mike came in.

"Mike, what is it?" I asked.

He sat down slowly in the chair facing me across the desk. "I'm sorry, Sheila. I have to ask you if you recognize the writing."

As he had done once before, he took out a plastic wallet from his pocket and laid it on the desk before me.

"It's okay," he said in response to my inquiring look. "It's been checked for fingerprints."

I took the envelope out of the wallet. It was addressed to Linda. The writing was Gina's.

"Yes," I said, "it's her handwriting. Was it . . . ?"

"It was beside her on the seat of the car," he said.

I looked at the envelope again. "I suppose she wrote it to Linda because she hasn't got any sort of family."

"No one at all?" he asked.

"No," I replied. "Her parents are dead, and there were no brothers or sisters. She didn't make friends easily. I think she had a very lonely life until she met Rebecca. That's why it was so important to her, I suppose. Poor Gina."

I turned the envelope over. It had been opened.

"Can I read it?" I asked.

"Sure," Mike said. "I think you should see what she says."

I took the letter out of the envelope and read it. It began abruptly.

I can't go on. There's no point in anything anymore now that Rebecca's gone, not my thesis or my life. Please tell Sheila I'm sorry.

Everyone must know what Loring did to Rebecca, so she had to kill herself. She couldn't

*bear it there any longer, and there was noth-
ing else she could do. Everyone must know
ke killed her; please tell them that. He killed
Rebecca, and it was only right he should be
killed, too. It was only justice. When I looked
down and saw him lying there, I was so glad.
It won't bring Rebecca back, I know that, but
it's only right he should be dead, too.*

*Please ask Gerda if she'll take my cat. I'm
sorry.*

Gina

I laid the letter down on the desk. It seemed as
if I could almost feel the pain and hopelessness
in the very texture of the paper.

"Oh, God," I said, "how terrible."

I felt the tears come into my eyes, tears for
Gina's desolation, tears, too, for the reference to
her thesis and to me. Gina's work had meant a
great deal to her, but it hadn't been enough.

"Yes," Mike said. "Poor kid."

He folded up the letter and put it into the
envelope.

"I guess this just about wraps it up," he said.
"Carl Loring's death."

"Carl Loring's . . . ." I echoed stupidly. "Oh! You
mean . . . ?"

"Well," Mike said, "it reads like a confession of
murder to me."

"Yes," I said slowly, "yes, I suppose it does."

"I've been making a few more inquiries since this was found," he went on. "And that man Johnson, Rick Johnson, says he saw her earlier on the morning Loring was killed. He says she was asking if he'd seen Loring anyplace. He thought she must have had bad news because she looked as if she'd been crying."

"She had," I said. "That was the morning she heard about Rebecca."

"And it was Loring's fault that Rebecca Long had to leave Wilmot?" Mike asked.

"Yes." I explained the circumstances of Rebecca's departure and the bad time she'd had afterwards. "I suppose, in a way, he was responsible for Rebecca's death," I said. "I can understand why Gina must have thought so."

"You didn't tell me." Mike looked at me quizzically.

"I honestly didn't make that sort of connection. I would have said Gina was the last person in the world to resort to that sort of violence. She was so quiet. . . ."

"Still waters . . ." Mike said. "You can never tell what a person's capable of if the provocation's strong enough. Poor kid," he repeated. "What a lousy business."

"I wonder why she waited until now to kill herself," I said.

"Getting up the nerve, I guess," Mike replied.

"She'd have been in shock for a couple of days after the killing."

"Linda spoke to her on the phone," I said. "She said she sounded terrible. Gina said she had a virus. . . . And all that time she was thinking about killing herself. If only we'd known!"

"What good would it have done?" Mike put the plastic wallet back in his pocket. "You wouldn't have wanted her to stand trial for murder."

"No," I said. "Of course not. I suppose this is the best solution all round, though it seems like a horrible thing to say."

We sat in silence for a while.

"Can I tell Linda?" I asked.

"People will have to know she's dead," Mike said, "but just for the moment I don't want anyone to know about the letter. Except your friend Linda. The letter was written to her. Ask her if she'll come around to see me. We need to keep the letter, of course, as evidence, but she'll want to read it for herself."

I fiddled with some of the student papers on my desk, piling one on top of the other, as if reducing them to order might somehow impose a similar order upon the whole sorry mess.

"So if Gina killed Carl Loring," I asked, "who killed Max?"

Mike rose from his chair. "I'm still waiting for a report to come in," he said, "but I figure I should be able to tell you that by Sunday."

* * *

Linda was very shocked by the news when I told her.

"If only she'd said something when I called!" she kept saying. "Just shut up in her apartment brooding about that terrible thing she'd done. That and Rebecca!"

"You mustn't blame yourself," I said gently. "There's nothing any of us could have done. It's better this way."

Tiger, sensing her mood, jumped up onto her lap and butted her hand with his head. She sat stroking the soft fur automatically for a while, and then she said, "I wonder if she was there, in the kitchen, when I went into the common room?"

"I suppose she might have been," I said. "She could have got out through the furnace room door. No one saw her in the corridor or anywhere around."

"I guess we'll never know," Linda said. "Oh, poor Gina! What she must have gone through to be driven to do such an awful thing; it doesn't bear thinking of! If only I'd made some sort of inquiries about Rebecca, kept in touch with her, tried to help, then maybe none of this would have happened."

"Linda," I said firmly, "you must stop thinking like that. There was nothing you could have done; you couldn't have changed anything."

* * *

The news of Gina's death, so soon after that of the Lorings, cast a gloom over the department. The atmosphere was decidedly low-key, and no one seemed to have the inclination for the usual academic infighting or points scoring.

"I've never known a committee meeting go so quickly and so smoothly," Dave Hunter said as we sat drinking coffee in Linda's room. "Everyone just said the minimum of what they had to say and we took a vote and that was that. Couldn't believe it—all over in half an hour!"

"I suppose we're all still in a state of shock," Linda said. "People just want to get on quietly with their work without any sort of hassle."

"Yeah, even O'Brien," Dave said. "She was positively conciliatory about the funding for the new publications program. And the egregious Rick hardly opened his mouth. I guess he's feeling lost without Loring to back him up."

"I certainly noticed a difference in our esteemed chair," Linda said, and I was pleased to hear the return of her old caustic tone. "Would you say '*accommodating*' was the word?"

"Definitely!" Dave smiled. "You know, I think we're going to be able to fix the whole of next year's course offerings without the usual casuistical rubbish, self-seeking, and empire building that we've had to put up with in recent years."

I got up. "I must leave you two to set Wilmot to right," I said. "I've got a conference with Sam in ten minutes. To be honest, I'm not looking forward to it. I'm afraid she's bound to be very upset about Gina."

Sam certainly didn't look her usual vital self. Her careful makeup couldn't wholly disguise the dark shadows under her eyes, and there was a listlessness about her that seemed to quench the brightness and vivacity that normally surrounded her like a sort of nimbus. Even the diamonds on her fingers appeared to have lost their sparkle.

"I'm so sorry, Sam," I said. "I know that you and Gina were very close."

"I should have guessed how it would be," she said quietly, "when I heard about Rebecca. I knew she couldn't live without her. But I was too wrapped up in my own affairs. I guess I can't forgive myself for that."

It seemed we all felt in some way responsible for Gina's death, a sort of collective guilt. However much we try to believe in fate and predestined laws, there's always the nagging feeling, deep down, that we, imperfect and human though we may be, could somehow prevent the tragedies of life. If only . . . Perhaps the two most futile words in the English language, but how often we find ourselves saying them.

"You mustn't think like that," I said. "It was no one's fault."

"It was that scumbag Loring's fault," Sam said vehemently. "If he hadn't persecuted Rebecca like that, none of this would have happened. At least he's dead, too—"

She broke off and looked at me. "I keep thinking. About Gina and Loring. She must have done it."

I shrugged my shoulders slightly but didn't say anything.

"You think so, too, don't you?" Sam persisted.

"Look, Sam," I replied hesitantly, "I can't say anything, but yes, it looks as if Gina did kill him. So, you see, things have turned out—not for the best, but you know what I mean."

"I suppose so," she replied. "It's all so complicated and such a terrible *waste*."

"I think you must all try and put it behind you," I said. "Get on with your lives. There's nothing more anyone can do. It's up to the police now to clear up the mess."

Sunday morning was clear and sunny, though quite cold, so we were glad of the heater in Mike's car as we drove from Harrisburg, past the Hershey factory with the smell of chocolate in the air, along Route 81 towards Hagerstown. By common consent we didn't mention the murders or Gina's death; instead Mike told me about Antietam and the battle that was fought there.

"I guess it was the turning point of the war," he said. "Lee wanted to take the fighting across the Union's southern border and have a kind of showdown battle. He didn't make it though he came darned close, even, but he had less than half the troops McClellan had. He was an extraordinary guy, McClellan, a kind of Hamlet figure, never quite able to make up his mind to act, always—what's that thing in *Macbeth*?—'Letting "I dare not" wait upon "I would." ' He never could bring himself to believe he had the advantage and always held back at the critical moment. . . ."

The battlefield was laid out like a great park, beautifully kept, the landmarks of the battle set out on plaques, telling where each division had stood and fought. There were many touching monuments to the dead, raised by survivors from the state they had come from.

"My father's great-grandfather fought under Grant at Spotsylvania," Mike said, "and my mother's great-grandfather was with Jackson at Harpers Ferry. I guess it was the same with you in England in your Civil War."

We walked along the sunken lane, bordered by zigzagged wooden post and rail fences, where so many soldiers had fallen, and stood silently outside the little white Dunker church which had been used as a hospital for the uncounted wounded. We stayed for a long time by the cornfield where the battle had raged so fiercely. We had seen very few people as we drove around the battlefield, and here we were completely alone. "It's stupid of me," I said, "but I've always thought of it as an English cornfield—you know, wheat. I hadn't realized that it would be maize and shoulder-high."

It was still a cornfield, the crop cut earlier but with a few straggling heads of corn left round the edges. The air was still, and there was no birdsong. The dead seemed very close.

When we stood on the bridge across Antietam Creek, where General Burnside had sent wave after wave of his men to their deaths, Mike said, "Nearly thirty thousand men were killed or wounded on that single day. More than on any battlefield where Americans have fought, before or since.

"It puts into perspective, I suppose, the deaths of the Lorings and Gina," I said, finally introducing the topic that was still on our minds.

"Yes," he replied, "I guess it does."

"You said you could tell me about Max Loring's death," I said. "Was it Carl who killed him?"

"Yes. It seems that he needed a lot of money, and Max wouldn't help."

"Just for this theater project?" I asked.

Mike was silent for a moment, looking at the water flowing under the bridge.

"No," he said finally. "It wasn't for that."

"What, then?" I asked impatiently. "What was so urgent that he needed so much?"

"Carl Loring had AIDS," Mike said.

For a moment I couldn't take in what Mike had said. Yes, of course, I knew all about AIDS; the papers and television often appeared to be full of nothing else. But suddenly to come upon it in this very immediate way seemed incredible.

"Are you sure?" I asked.

"It's one of the first things they look for in a postmortem," Mike said. "You can't be too careful these days."

"No one at Wilmot had the faintest idea," I said.

"It seems to have been in the early stages." Mike went on. "He must have taken it very badly, got really scared. He was trying everything he could find, anything for some miracle cure—alternative medicine, quack clinics, and all that stuff. It doesn't come cheap."

"And Max wouldn't help him?" I asked.

"I guess not. We found a letter from Max in Carl's desk which more or less said he'd made his bed and he could damn well lie on it."

"How awful!" I exclaimed. "How could he? His own brother!"

"I guess the money from the sale of the family house was the last straw. Carl must have felt he had a right to a share of that."

"He could have gone to law," I suggested.

"The law can take a while," Mike replied. "He didn't think he had the time. Anyhow, after the lawyers had been at it, there wouldn't have been that much left!"

"He must have been desperate," I said.

Much as I had disliked Carl Loring, I couldn't help feeling how terrible his situation had been and how the despair must have eaten away at him as time passed and the disease proceeded inexorably.

"I suppose, after that row he had with his brother," I said, "he came early for the concert and found Max upstairs alone in the study room—I don't suppose there'd have been many people around at that time of day—and shot him."

"He was unlucky in one way," Mike said. "When he put his brother's body in that blanket chest, he must have thought no one would find it for quite a while. It was just by chance that Theo Portman chose to show you around the institute that evening and even more by chance that he took you up to show you the top floor and that linen storage stuff."

"That's true. I don't expect Theo usually took visitors up there. But look," I said as a thought struck me, "if Max's body wasn't found, then how would Carl get at the money? I mean, he couldn't inherit until people knew his brother was dead."

"If he'd inherited in the usual way," Mike replied, "and he was his brother's heir, then it would have taken time, and that, we know he didn't have. But if Carl said that Max had gone away—he often went on trips abroad, sometimes on the spur of the moment—then Carl would have access to his papers and so forth and could forge his signature. It looks like he'd done that once before."

"Good heavens!" I exclaimed. "How do you know?"

"He'd kept a letter from Max threatening him with the law if he did it again. Saying he'd put up with the scandal to get even."

"What a pair!" I said.

"Anyway," Mike said, "it all seems to fit together. I figure we can make a good case for Carl Loring murdering his brother."

"Yes," I said slowly, "it does seem to be the only explanation."

"I'll be glad to get it cleared up," Mike said. "It's been a messy, unsatisfactory affair."

"Yes," I agreed, thinking that it would be more comfortable now I need no longer feel I was keeping from Mike things he ought to know about my friends at Wilmot. "It's been that, all right!"

I leaned forward and rested my arms on the bridge, looking out at the trees lining the sloping ground on either side of the creek. They still retained some shreds of leaves, which conjured up melancholy images of a tattered, retreating army.

"Mike," I asked, "what's that faint smell? Sort of sweet and musky?"

He looked down. "The coping of the bridge is covered with cedarwood," he said.

"Cedarwood!"

I was back again in that bleak room with the

body of a man neatly lying in a cedarwood box as though in a coffin. Here countless men had died, in the water or on the cold ground, not neatly but horribly mangled, limbs torn, scattered pieces of humanity, coffinless. The sweet smell hung in the air like the smell of death. Max Loring's death already seemed remote, far away; it would soon be forgotten. The deaths here would not be forgotten. I looked over the bridge at the creek flowing below and wondered how long it would take for the water to wash away the blood.

14

The semester was drawing to a close, and I was looking forward to going home.

"Anna will be down for a couple of days tomorrow," Linda said. "There's some stuff she needs to do at the institute before the vacation. Then we'll all have a week in New York before you go. How does that sound?"

"Oh, lovely. I can do my Christmas shopping in Macy's and Bloomingdale's; it'll solve all my problems. Even the simplest present seems glamorous if it's come from abroad!"

The revelation about Carl Loring shook the department badly. People seemed disinclined to talk about it or about Gina. It was as though they wanted to pretend the whole thing had never happened. Gradually the factions were reformed, the battle lines were redrawn, but there was less confrontation; the former rancor was gone.

"You wouldn't believe," Linda said, "the way Rob Huron was actually *congratulating* Dave on his new syllabus for freshman comp for next year! After all the fighting we've had to get anything like it!"

"I believe you're missing the battles," I said with amusement.

"No way! I tell you, Sheila, I still can't get used to waking up in the morning and actually looking forward to going in!"

I'd finished my last class and said good-bye (with genuine regret) to my students and was in the process of clearing up generally. I always seem to accumulate an enormous amount of odds and ends, even in a short time, and I'm also an absolute fool about throwing things away. Silly things, like a paper napkin printed with the name and logo of the Blue Diner, for instance, or my name tag from a special seminar. Michael might be interested to see them, I tell myself, knowing full well that he won't. No, it's just that I can't bear to shed any bit of my life. I've got museum ticket stubs from all over the world; they fall out of books and send me into time-wasting fits of nostalgia and reverie. I'd just taken some books back to the library and felt I needed a cup of coffee so I went into the common room kitchen. I switched on the coffee machine, took the tube of sweeteners out of my bag, and put them on the work top while I got a mug out of the cupboard. As I moved to turn the machine off, I knocked the sweeteners onto the floor, and they rolled under the fridge. Rather stiffly I got down onto my knees to look for them. They'd rolled right under the gap beneath the fridge, and I had to find a knife to fish for them. As I eased them out, something else came with them. It was a ballpoint pen. I stood up and took it over to the light to see what was written on it. For a moment its significance didn't register with me. Then, as the realization of what I'd found was gradually borne in upon me, I put the pen in my bag and went away, all thoughts of coffee forgotten.

"Anna's skipped breakfast," Linda said next morning. "She said she pigged out yesterday at some fabulous new Italian restaurant in the Village, masses of polenta fried in butter and stuff like that. Anyway, she's gone off jogging—*with* her weights on!—and she'll go straight to the institute. She'll see you this evening, and we'll make plans."

I'd been out when Anna arrived the night before, having a farewell dinner with Sam and Hal. I, too, after being exposed to the full glory of Sam's cooking, didn't feel much like breakfast.

"I think I'll just have juice and coffee," I said cautiously. "I don't think I'm going to be able to face food for several days!"

"Did Sam do her famous crab cakes?" Linda asked, laughing.

"She did," I replied, "each one a meal in itself.

There were *two* of those, and then we had some sort of Cajun chicken *and* pecan pie. I honestly don't know *how* I got home!"

"Isn't it today you're having lunch with the Sterns?" Linda asked.

"Oh, God! I'd forgotten. Oh, well, I'll just have to toy lightly with a salad or something. I've got to go into the department and collect the last of my things, so if I go now, I might have time for a brisk walk by the river to work off last night's excesses before lunch!"

In my office I packed the last remaining papers into my briefcase and put a strap round the books. I picked up my coffee mug, emblazoned with the words "Wilmot Giants" and an American football helmet, and went along to the common room kitchen to rinse it out.

As I opened the door, I saw a figure in a gray tracksuit crouched on the floor, apparently searching for something.

"Is this what you're looking for, Anna?" I asked, taking the ballpoint pen from my bag.

"Sheila!" Anna got to her feet and came towards me. Something in my face made her stop. "Sheila, what is it?"

I held out the pen. "Chicopee Falls Motel," I said.

Somehow the ridiculous name made the whole thing seem even more unreal. "You must have got it when you were staying there for the conference, and there was no other time you could have lost it, was there? Only the day Carl Loring was killed. And you never said you'd been in here. Why was that?"

"I think you know why," Anna said quietly.

"I know when, and I know how," I said, "but I don't know why."

"Look, Sheila," Anna said urgently, "I have to explain. But not here, please."

"We'd better go to my office," I said.

We sat down facing each other across the desk. I found I was still stupidly clutching the coffee mug, so I put it down on the desk, slowly and with infinite care, as if it were made of the finest porcelain.

For a while neither of us spoke; then Anna said, "I don't know where to begin."

"Just tell me," I said. "Tell me what happened."

"I didn't mean to kill Carl," Anna said at last. "It was Max I had to get rid of."

"Max?" I was startled. "So Carl didn't kill his brother."

"No, I did. Max . . . he was responsible for Dan's death. I just found out."

"But surely . . ."

"Dan died in Vietnam? Oh, sure he did. But he wasn't killed by the Vietcong—well, he was, but the man really responsible for his death was Max Loring."

"How terrible!" I cried. "What happened?"

Anna took a deep breath and shook her head as if to clear it.

"Dan was an infantry officer, attached for this one mission to a reconnaissance group checking out enemy positions. They were ambushed by the Vietcong but managed to call up their helicopter by radio. Most of the group had been wounded in the ambush; only the officer in charge and the sergeant were unhurt. The helicopter managed to land in this paddy, but they were under really fierce Vietcong fire. The officer and sergeant rushed over and managed to scramble on board. They told the pilot to take off right away. They said everyone else had been killed." She was silent for a moment. "Dan was one of the wounded," she said, "left behind to be slaughtered by the Vietcong. The officer who got away—who left men to die to save his own skin—was Max Loring."

"Oh, Anna," I said, "I'm so sorry."

She was shivering, and her voice was very low so that I could hardly hear what she was saying. "I only found out quite recently. The sergeant, the other man who got away, was dying of lung cancer and had it on his conscience. He managed to find the relatives of the men who had died so that he could let them know what really happened. I wish"—her voice broke—"I wish I'd never known."

"Did you tell Linda?" I asked.

She shook her head. "I couldn't. It would have hurt her so much. I'm the eldest. It was my responsibility. I knew I had to act for the both of us. As soon as I found out how Dan had died, I couldn't think of anything else; it became an obsession, a sort of madness. I guess I knew I had to kill Max Loring. Nothing else would do; nothing else would free me from the horror I was feeling.

"I had Dan's old target pistol—he was really good; did I ever tell you he won a medal at Camp Penny?—and I sort of kept it after he died, though I never thought I'd use it." She gave a little laugh and went on, "I found Max Loring up in the computer room that day. It was quite late in the afternoon, so there was no one else around. He seemed surprised to see me. I said I knew about Vietnam, explained how I'd been told. He went quite white. It was odd; I've never seen anyone do that before. All the color drained right out of his face. He blustered a bit, but he was so scared. . . . I unslung my purse from my shoulder and dropped it onto the floor; then I took the pistol from my jacket pocket and shot him."

"Anna!"

"I didn't expect to get away with it. I thought people would come running when they heard the shot. But nobody came. And do you know, there was no blood; the bullet hadn't even come out the other side! I thought if I got away with it, Linda would never have to know about Dan. So I thought maybe I'd hide the body so that it wouldn't be found until I was back in New York. I remembered the old blanket chest; Theo was fond of showing it to people. Max wasn't heavy, just a little man, and I'm very strong. I got him into the chest and went away. I didn't see anyone, so I just left the building and came right back to change for the concert."

"And you'd left for New York," I said slowly, "when we found him. And of course, there seemed no reason for you to be involved. The police barely questioned you; there was no sort of motive."

"Your lieutenant called me on the telephone in New York," Anna said. "He seemed perfectly happy when I told him I'd been in the main galleries and not in the study rooms." We sat for a while in silence. I could barely take in what Anna had said: the horror of Dan's death, the calm way she had told me of Max Loring's murder. Eventually I asked, "What about Carl Loring?"

Anna got up and walked about the room. "As I told you," she said, "I didn't mean to kill Carl. I'd been jogging, remember, and I thought I'd come in and get a cup of coffee from Linda. I went into her room, but she wasn't there and her coffee machine wasn't working, so I went along to the common room."

"What time was this?" I asked.

"Just after ten, I guess," she replied. "I figured Linda had gone to a class or something. Anyway, I went into the kitchen and found Carl Loring there. I said something about coming in to bum a cup of coffee and he made some snide remark about people using the place like a coffee shop. I went to put my purse down on the table but I dropped it and it fell on the floor, scattering things all over. I felt like a fool, down on my knees, scrabbling about trying to get things together with him sneering at me. Then he bent down and picked something up. It was an empty cartridge case."

She gave a short laugh. "I couldn't believe it— when I shot Max Loring it hadn't occurred to me to look for the empty case. I didn't hear anything, you see, because it had fallen into my open purse there on the floor of the computer room. He stood over me with it in his hand, and when I scrambled to my feet he said very slowly, 'Is this some kind of souvenir? I think I should keep it. I believe they can match such things, and maybe this is from the bullet that killed my dear brother. Of course, I wouldn't dream of taking it to the police—not yet—there are all sorts of interesting things you and I might like to talk about first.' Then I knew he didn't care at all about his brother being killed. He was going to use it to blackmail me." She flung herself down into the chair facing me and said violently, "There was no way. . . . And besides, he was such a vile person and he'd made Linda so unhappy. Not just work, but all that business about Doug. And I knew he'd use this to get at her as well as me."

"You knew about Doug?" I asked, startled.

"Dave told me; he was so worried about her, though he made me promise not to let her know I knew. Oh, Carl Loring had made so *many* people miserable! That's how I justified it to myself later. At the time I guess it was a kind of blind panic. I snatched up the knife and killed him." She gave a shaky little laugh. "I guess Linda was right about my purse. If I'd cleaned it out when she asked me that day, the day I shot Max, I'd have found the cartridge case then and Carl Loring would still be alive. Crazy, isn't it?"

I seemed incapable of saying anything, and Anna went on, "I stood there for a while, just looking down at him; then I wiped the handle of the knife to get rid of my fingerprints and washed the blood off my hands at the sink. I was just going to leave when I heard someone come into the common room. For a moment I thought I was trapped, but then I tried the door that leads to the furnace room, and by some miracle it was unlocked, so I got out that way. There was no one around when I came out of the furnace room. I just ran all the way back to the institute. I was in my tracksuit, just another jogger back from a run. Josh, one of the guards, joked about it."

"It must have been Gina who came into the common room while you were in the kitchen," I said. "Then she went in there and found the body. . . . Of course! There wasn't anything in her note that said she had *killed* Carl Loring—just that she was glad when she saw him dead."

Anna looked stricken but didn't say anything.

"I suppose Linda told you that the police think Carl murdered his brother?" I said. "And that Gina killed Carl?"

Anna nodded.

"Did she tell you that Carl Loring had AIDS?" I asked.

Anna stared at me with horror in her eyes. She looked down at her hands. "Oh, my God," she said quietly. "That scratch on my hand from Tiger— remember? And Carl Loring's blood when I wiped the knife . . ."

I got up quickly and went and put my arms round her. "It may be all right, Anna," I said urgently. "You mustn't worry. There's only the faintest chance. . . ."

She clung to me for a moment, and then she got up, picked up her handbag, and slung it over her shoulder.

"It's all the same, really. I killed two people. I guess it's only fair there should be some kind of retribution." She gave a wry smile. "Of course, I don't know what you're going to do, Sheila. Will you tell your lieutenant?"

"No," I said. "No, how could I? Both Carl and Gina are dead. Neither of them has any family to be hurt if people go on thinking they were murderers."

Anna smiled. "That's a very partial kind of casuistry," she said.

"You're my friend," I said, "and so is Linda. I love you both very much. The Lorings and Gina are dead; nothing can bring them back. How could I condemn you to God knows what and break Linda's heart?"

Anna shook her head. "It isn't fair to ask you to make that kind of choice," she said. "But thank you all the same."

She came over and gave me a hug and said, "I'm going right back to New York."

"Today?" I asked.

"Yes," she replied, "right now. So this is goodbye."

"I'll see you in a few days, then," I said, "when Linda and I come up."

"Sure," she said. "I'll see you."

15

I don't know how I got through my lunch with the Sterns. I hope they put my abstraction down to excitement at going back to England. We parted with many earnest promises to meet at wherever place in England they found themselves attending a conference. ("It'll either be Feminism and Semiotics at Bristol or Cognitive Research on Gender and Comprehension at Cambridge. I guess we're going to need a little relief after either of those!") Yet I was glad of their company. My thoughts were in a turmoil, and I found myself putting off the moment when I would have to face Linda and Anna.

But by the time I got back Anna had already gone.

"She had an urgent call," Linda said. "Someone in her department was sick, so she had to chair some committee or other. We'll see her in Brooklyn Heights in a couple of days."

I found it difficult to talk to Linda with Anna's

dreadful secret uppermost in my mind, so I said I wanted to do a bit of packing and went to my room straight after supper. I was just persuading Tiger, who had followed me, not to take up residence in the suitcase I had opened on my bed, when the telephone rang. I could hear Linda go to answer it, and after a short while she came into my room.

"Sheila," she said, and her voice was hoarse and almost unrecognizable. "Something terrible has happened."

"What is it?" I asked anxiously.

"It's Anna—she's—she's been in a car crash. They say she's dead."

Linda sank onto a chair and buried her face in her hands.

"Oh, no!" I knelt beside the chair, attempting to comfort her as she tried to speak through her sobs.

"It was some hospital in New Jersey," she said. "That's where they took her. I don't know what happened. I must go to her."

"Yes, yes, of course," I said, "and I'll come with you, of course. But look, why don't I phone Mike and see if he can find out for us what's happened?"

Mike rang back after a little while. "I've been on to the New Jersey police," he said. "It seems she simply lost control—just went off the road. Lost her concentration, maybe. It happens. No other vehicle was involved."

Mike was wonderful. He drove us to the hospital, saw to all the police formalities, and brought us back to Allenbrook again just as dawn was breaking.

"Have you got a sleeping pill to give her?" he asked.

"Yes," I replied wearily. "I've got something."

"I think you should take a couple yourself," he said, looking at me critically. "You look almost as bad as Linda."

But no pills could bring me rest as I turned over and over in my mind what I knew and what had happened. And what, most of all, should I do? It seemed fairly certain that Anna had deliberately crashed her car. Of course, I couldn't tell Linda what had passed between Anna and me. Not only would she have to face the agonizing reality of what Anna had done and why—all the trauma of her brother's death revived tenfold—but she would then be sure, as I was, that Anna had taken her own life. Linda had enough to bear without any of that. No, I couldn't tell her. But was it fair, now that Anna was dead, not to tell Mike what had really happened? My conscience told me I should, but the thought of an official statement that Linda would have to know about made it equally impossible to tell him. After tossing and turning for a few hours, I gave up and got up. I found Linda in the kitchen.

"I'm sorry," she said, "I did try to sleep, but—well, I couldn't."

I made us some coffee, and we sat for a while in silence.

"Thank God you're here," Linda said suddenly. "I don't think I could have borne it if you hadn't been here."

I felt a dreadful pang of guilt. If I hadn't been here, I wouldn't have found the pen, and Anna might still have been alive.

That was my predominant feeling throughout the next few days. Anna's body was brought back to Allenbrook, and she was buried, not in the graveyard of the little Moravian church, beside the Revolutionary soldier and the Mohican but in one of the new cemeteries where the gravestones went right down to the pavement.

The evening before I left Allenbrook I had dinner with Mike. "The first thing I'm going to do when I retire next year is buy a plane ticket to England," he said. "Will you show me around Stratford-upon-Avon?"

"Yes," I said smiling. "We'll stand on Clopton Bridge and look at the swans."

"I'm sorry your time in Allenbrook had to be spoiled by all that's happened," he said, "but, then again, if it hadn't been that way, I guess we would never have met, and that would have been a shame."

"A great shame."

"It's been a strange kind of case, but it ended neatly enough, I guess."

"Yes," I replied.

"Very neatly," Mike said. "Unless," he continued, looking at me quizzically, "there's something I've missed?"

Perhaps I paused a moment too long before saying, "No, what else could there be?" because he looked at me rather sadly, almost as if he knew that I hadn't been honest with him.

"You'll be glad to be back home with your son and those animals you've told me about," he said, and we talked of other things, but at the end of the evening, in spite of reiterated plans to meet in England, we parted with something like constraint between us, and I was sorry, because he was a nice man and I couldn't help feeling that I'd treated him less than fairly.

Linda drove me straight to Kennedy Airport from Allenbrook. We neither of us felt like staying in New York. As we said good-bye, she clung to me. "Thank you again for everything, Sheila. Thank you for helping me deal with things."

We were both crying. I found I couldn't say anything.

I'd been given a seat by the window, but in my usual nervous state I carefully didn't look out as the plane took off. My mind was still in a state of turmoil. I was pretty sure that Mike suspected that the neat solution to the deaths of Max and Carl Loring was not the right one. Whether he had thought about Anna's death and put two and two together I wasn't sure. Certainly he had no means of knowing why Anna had killed them, and without a motive there was nothing he could do. Linda was safe. It was all for the best, I kept telling myself. This way the hurt was kept to a minimum; nothing could undo what had been done. Surely it was best to leave things as they were. And yet . . .

The pilot's voice came over the intercom and broke into my thoughts. For a moment I didn't take in what he was saying, something about an engine fault and having to return to New York.

"We'll have to cruise around a bit to use up some fuel," the voice was saying. "The stewards will be round with drinks."

There was a moment's silence and then a buzz of conversation. I looked out of the window. Somehow I wasn't nervous now.

We were flying up the coast, each inlet perfectly defined as on a map. The pilot's voice again, bracing and cheerful: "It never rains, but it pours! I'm afraid we have a problem with the undercarriage, so we'll be landing with the emergency gear."

The woman sitting beside me crossed herself, but there appeared to be no signs of panic. A little way up the aisle I saw some of the cabin staff bizarrely jumping up and down, presumably in an effort to shake the undercarriage loose. None of it seemed at all real. I found I wasn't frightened. It seemed inconceivable that I might die, that I might never see Michael again. I looked out of the window again. The skyline of Manhattan was spread out below, the fairy-tale towers of the skyscrapers looking as magical as they did in all the photographs. And just as unreal. We were coming in now and over the airport. I could see ambulances and fire engines racing out to the runway, but it seemed impossible that they might be for us.

We were approaching the runway. Instinctively I shut my eyes and held my breath. There was a slight jarring movement and the grinding sound of wheels on tarmac, then a deceleration and the great plane taxied almost demurely along the ground and we were safely down. Spontaneously all the passengers applauded, broad smiles of relief and congratulation, to the pilot for his skill, to each other for still being alive. I found that I was crying.

In the passenger lounge I knew immediately what I had to do. As I queued for one of the telephones, I searched in my bag for the telephone number of Mike's office. I had been given a second chance. Fate had made up my mind for me. I was going to clear my conscience.

"Hello, can I speak to Lieutenant Landis, please? It's urgent."

The voice at the other end was polite but disinterested. "I'm sorry. The lieutenant isn't here right now. He's had to go to Pittsburgh on an inquiry. Would you care to leave a message?"

"No," I said. "No message. Thank you."

I sat down and opened my book and waited for the replacement plane that would take me home.

The Cruellest Month

The death of spinster Gwen Richmond seemed excessively nasty even for a most unlikable woman. Her fatal burial under a collapsed shelf of rare books had forced the Bodleian Library to close and cast a pall over the university's sweet April days. Still, Mrs. Malory was shocked to find out that so many people were openly glad the librarian was dead. Widow Sheila Malory had come up to Oxford for a little scholarly research and a lot of happy reminiscing about her college years. Instead, her natural affinity for uncovering things suspicious and sinister soon cast a dark shadow over her own rosy colored memories ... and chilled her to the bone when she discovered that Gwen Richmond had not died by accident, but because someone had a desperate motive to kill her.

Mrs. Malory and The Festival Murder

Character assassinations take place daily in genteel Taviscombe, particularly between longtime residents and upstart newcomers. But genuine bloody murder almost never happens in the cozy English village—until the Taviscombe Festival. Sometime between the dulcet madrigal and the scrumptious buffet served at stately Kinsford Manor, someone bludgeons local poet and insufferable literary lion Adrian Palgrave to death. Mrs. Sheila Malory feels especially shaken by the discovery. Her knowledge of village animosities tells her a long list of suspects live uncomfortably close to home. Now that the high-strung and universally hated Adrian is dead, the wife he flagrantly cheated on is behaving oddly, and the TV producer whose secrets he threatened to expose seems to be gloating. Yet it is one unexpected bit of gossip that puts Mrs. Malory herself in danger . . . as if she may know too much for a desperate killer to bear.

Mrs. Malory's Shortest Journey

Sheila Malory loves visiting the West Lodge Nursing Home, where she can catch up on all the local gossip with resident Mrs. Jankiewicz. The latest scandal is that wealthy widow Edith Rossiter's scheming daughter, Thelma, is pressuring her to sign over a substantial amount of money against her wishes. Sheila suspects the worst when Mrs. Rossiter disappears after a shopping trip. A search of her room reveals that her sleeping pills are missing, and reports soon arise that a mysterious man and woman were seen talking to Mrs. Rossiter shortly before her disappearance. With no hard evidence to back up Sheila's suspicions of foul play, further investigations reach a dead end. It is only when Michael, Sheila's son, makes a chance discovery while researching in the library that Sheila uncovers the key to the whole mystery. However, the truth is more surprising than Mrs. Malory could ever have imagined.